Iron Pot Bob's Catch and Eat Cookbook

Bob Kawka

Bob Kawka

Copyright © 2025 by Bob Kawka

ISBN: 978-1-966642-74-9

Dedication

To the unsung cooks who spend countless hours planning and preparing great dishes for others.

Bob Kawka

Acknowledgement

I acknowledge the countless hours of proofreading, taste testing, and critiquing of my culinary ideas that my wife, Iron Skillet Elaine, put into this book, and Shaina, New York Publishers, for patiently guiding me through "real-world" publishing.

Table of Contents

About the Author

Bob first started learning to cook while earning his Boy Scout cooking merit badge. Then things kind of got out of hand. With both parents being great cooks, they expected him to learn more than the basic requirements of the merit badge. He had to learn how to plan a meal, purchase the ingredients, and prepare the family meals. Along the way, Bob and Elaine became certified kitchen supervisors with the American Red Cross. Because he wanted to share many of the wonderful recipes he encountered throughout his cooking journey, Bob wrote three cookbooks. Two were written for Dutch oven cooks, and one focused on ways to cook the fabulous Florida seafood around his home in Daytona Beach, Florida. He occasionally conducts a Dutch oven cooking school when he's not scouting out new recipes.

Introduction

I started this cookbook because many members of our fishing club knew how to catch fish, but when it came to cooking their catch, that was another story.

Many excuses were given for not cooking: "It's too messy." "I don't know how to cook that fish." Other reasons for not cooking were, "My spouse doesn't like fish." And the list goes on.

Once I started showing that there is life beyond frying, people started eating more of what they caught.

In the South, the traditional ways of cooking seafood are frying or making a type of seafood stew called a *gumbo* or a *jambalaya*, which is a gumbo with rice. Baking is the other standby.

Iron Skillet and I started on a quest to expand the seafood cooking knowledge of folks by encouraging them to try more variety, like BBQ, smoking, or poaching their seafood. We tried to keep our recipes as simple as possible, as we would rather spend our time eating rather than cooking. We tried to shy away from exotic spices and herbs.

In the appendix, starting on page 96, we have included some of the "little things" that come up during cooking our dishes.

If you are looking to get really fancy, here are three of our favorite cookbooks.

- <u>The Ultimate Fish and Shellfish Cookbook</u> by Kate Whiteman. This may be out of print, but it is well worth it if you can find it, since it has a lot of wonderful seafood recipes.

- <u>School of Fish</u> by Ben Pollinger. Besides a lot of professional-grade fancy recipes, Mr. Pollinger does a lot of teaching about various seafood and cooking techniques.
- <u>Ralph Brennan's New Orleans Seafood Cookbook</u> by Ralph Brennan. Where else would you find great seafood but in New Orleans? This cookbook uses both Creole and Cajun cooking techniques to create simple but unique New Orleans recipes.

There are many more wonderful cookbooks out there. So don't be bashful about looking in the cookbook section of your favorite bookstore or checking out yard sales and second-hand stores, where you may find some great cookbooks at very reasonable prices. The other place where there are literally millions of recipes is the internet."

When we find a recipe that we have tried and like, we copy or print it out and put it in a ring binder, along with notes, to use again. We are currently at 21 full-ring binders, but who's counting?

We have tried to leave space at the end of each recipe for your notes so you can personalize the recipe to your tastes. We have used a bigger font size to make it easier to read while cooking.

Enough jawing about why we did these recipes. Let's get cooking!

Bob Kawka, AKA Iron Pot Bob

Elaine Kawka, AKA Iron Skillet Elaine

To Begin With

Step 1: Catch a fish, dig some clams, catch some crabs, or dig oysters. If the fish isn't biting or you need more, look around for a reputable fish market. Be sure to check the origin of your fish or seafood. If it's from countries like China, Vietnam, or Korea, be aware that they are rumored to raise their seafood under questionable conditions. Local wild-caught is better than farm-raised, but it is usually more expensive. However, knowing what seafood is in season can mean fresher and cheaper products. Here in Florida, we are spoiled between both coasts. There are over 26 different kinds of saltwater seafood, plus a bountiful supply of freshwater seafood. For those poor, unfortunate people who live elsewhere, a good fishmonger can usually get you a particular fish if it's in season and you are willing to pay for it.

Step 2: Select a recipe and read it completely, then assemble all the ingredients before you start cooking. How many times have you been in the middle of cooking a magnificent feast and found you were out of a key spice or ingredient? Just make sure you have everything before you start.

Step 3: Cook. Anytime you first cook a recipe, we suggest that you follow it as written and make notes as to how your family wants it prepared next time.

Appetizers

Crab Meat Newburg Appetizer

Here is another of our favorite appetizers. It is a little pricier and takes a bit longer to prepare, but it's a good holiday dish for those "special" parties.

Ingredients:

- 2 tablespoons butter
- 2 tablespoons flour
- ½ teaspoon sea salt
- 2 cups milk
- 2 cups shredded cheddar cheese
- 2 cans (7 ½ ounces each) crab chunks, preferably Alaskan King crab, drained and flaked
- 3 hard-boiled eggs, grated or finely chopped
- ½ cup finely chopped onion
- 1 pinch of cayenne or red pepper
- 1 tablespoon parsley (for garnish)

Directions:

- Melt the butter in a saucepan over medium-high heat, then mix in the flour and salt. Next, gradually add the milk, stirring until the mixture is thickened and smooth.
- Add cheese, stirring until blended. Then, blend in the remaining ingredients except parsley.

- Pour the mixture into a 1½ quart casserole and bake at 325°F for about 15 minutes until heated through. We like to use a rapid-read digital thermometer to make sure the inside has reached at least 150° or more.
- Remove from the oven, sprinkle the parsley on top, and let everything sit for a few minutes to blend.

Since this is an appetizer, you can get as fancy as you want by dishing the mixture into individual small bowls and serving with Melba toast rounds or toast points. Otherwise, just leave it in the casserole and let everybody help themselves.

Notes: ____

____

____

____

____

____

____

Ceviche

Ingredients:

- 1 pound medium shrimp, peeled and deveined
- ½ pound of Bay scallops (that's those little ones)
- 4 ounces each of fresh lemon juice and lime juice
- 6 ounces of orange juice
- 1 hothouse cucumber that is peeled and seeded. Then chop into ½ inch cubes or about the size of your Bay scallops.
- ½ cup of finely chopped red onion
- Up to ½ cup of finely chopped chilies, depending on your taste. I like to use Serrano chilies, but you can use your favorite hot chilies instead.
- 1 cup of seeded and diced fresh tomatoes
- 1 tablespoon of cilantro (or more if you want to make it hotter). Note: The cilantro also makes a nice garnish if you're serving it to your in-laws.
- If you want to go extra fancy, chop up an avocado into cubes the same size as your cucumber (about a half-inch cube).

Directions:

- First, cut the shrimp into 1/2-inch chunks. Then, put the shrimp, scallops, cucumber, red onion, and chilies into a glass or stainless-steel bowl.
- Pour the citrus juices over everything and mix well. Let your mixture sit at room temperature for about ½ hour before chilling. (This lets the citrus juices "cook" the ingredients.)

- About an hour or so before you are ready to serve, remove the bowl from the refrigerator and add the tomatoes, avocado, and cilantro. Mix well and chill again.
- Just before serving, taste. You may or may not want to add salt and/or more cilantro.

This recipe should make about six servings. If you want to get fancy, chill whatever you're going to serve and garnish with cilantro. Since this is a good hot weather dish, you will want to serve something cold to drink.

Note: The following wine was "officially" tasted and found to pair well with this recipe. Bellini Frascati 2015 (Rufina, Italy). Described as crisp, with hints of tree fruit and floral notes.

Notes: ____

____

____

____

____

____

IPB's Crab Appetizer

When one is retired or not fishing, one watches TV. Guess what Iron Pot watches? Food shows, what else? Saw this on a show called "The Chew." Didn't get all the ingredients, so had to add my own touches.

Ingredients:

- 1 can (16 ounces) lump crab meat or 1 pound of Alaskan King crab meat, coarsely chopped
- ⅔ cup very thinly cut celery
- ¼ cup chives, thinly cut
- 1 stick of butter
- 1 teaspoon celery seed, not celery salt
- 1 teaspoon smoked paprika
- 1 tablespoon yellow mustard
- 1 slice of raclette cheese cut approximately ½ inch thick
- 1 loaf of French bread, hand-cut into ½ inch slices (start with 6 slices)

Directions:

- Lightly toast the bread slices in the oven under the broiler.
- Melt the butter in a 2-quart pot over medium-low heat.
- Melt the slice of cheese in a small pan over medium heat.
- Add the celery, paprika, and mustard to the butter and gently mix for 3 minutes (just so the spices can mingle a bit).

- Gently fold the crab lumps into the butter mixture and heat over medium heat for about 3 to 5 minutes (check the crab to make sure it's heated all the way through).
- Generously spoon the crab mixture onto a toasted slice.
- Then spread the melted cheese over the top of the mixture on the bread slice and serve with the beverage of your choice. (Remember that the cook chooses what to drink. Of course, the cook may have to first sample the various drink possibilities to find what will go best with this appetizer.)

This can be eaten by hand or, if you want to be formal, use a knife and fork. Some cooks will sprinkle a little paprika (for presentation) or cayenne (to make it spicier) over the top of the cheese.

Any leftover mixture, when heated, goes really well over poached eggs on toasted muffins for a fancy brunch or breakfast.

Note: As always, a chilled mild white wine like a Pinot Grigio or a Chardonnay will enhance your dining experience (and impress your relatives).

Notes: ____

____

____

____

____

Slavek's Fish Dip

We caught Mr. Slavek, the Executive Chef at Down the Hatch Restaurant, in a good moment, and he graciously shared his famous dip recipe with us.

Ingredients and Directions:

- Start with King Mackerel pieces (usually at least a pound) that have been filleted.
- Sprinkle with seasoned salt (y'all might try seasoned salt that has some sugar in it).
- Put the pieces in a pan and cook on the grill or smoker. Add some water to the pan for steam as the fish cooks. This way, the fish doesn't get a crust on it.
- Put the fish in a large bowl and chop it up.
- Add 1/8 teaspoon or more freshly ground pepper and ½ cup mayonnaise. Stir.
- Add a heaping tablespoon each of finely chopped celery and onion.
- Start with 1 tablespoon of fresh lemon juice.
- Mix well, making sure all fish pieces are well blended into the mixture. If necessary, put on some food gloves and break up the fish pieces with your fingers so that they blend thoroughly with the rest of the ingredients.
- Chill for at least 45 minutes, then taste and adjust seasonings. You Southern Crackers may want to add some cayenne pepper to increase "the kick."
- Serve with your favorite beverage and crackers.

Smoked Amberjack Dip

Now, I know a lot of you have nothing else to do when you're retired except fish, party, and fish. Usually, when fishing and partying, you need to have something to eat along with your adult beverages. Here is a recap of a Smoked Amberjack Dip that Iron Skillet and I have demonstrated over the years to various groups.

Ingredients:

- ½ lb. smoked amberjack or smoked mullet
- ½ lb. softened cream cheese
- 1 heaping tablespoon of chopped celery
- 2 tablespoons chopped green pepper
- 2 heaping tablespoons chopped sweet onion
- 1 tablespoon fresh dill

Directions:

- Put all ingredients into a blender or food processor. If you have more fish, add more ingredients.
- Blend briefly in your blender or food processor. Or use a bowl and fork to whip it up the old-fashioned way.
- You may want to let the dip rest for a couple of hours for all the ingredients to get acquainted. Since this is your dip, adjust everything to fit your taste. (The cook gets to season it their way.)
- You may want to add just a bit of Old Bay Seasoning and/or red pepper/cayenne just to make it a little bit more southern.

- If it's too thick, mix in a bit of sour cream to thin it out.

You can store this dip in your refrigerator if you are going to use it in the next couple of days, or freeze it if you want to keep it for longer periods of time. However, it is best served at room temperature with your favorite crackers.

Note: Mrs. and I like to pair this dip with the following wine: Kitchen Sink White Table Wine (Santa Rosa, California). Described as a blend of Chardonnay, Chenin Blanc, and Gewurztraminer to create a beautifully balanced wine with melon and floral notes, a lush, fruity mouth feel, and a light, flinty finish.

Notes: ____

____

____

____

____

____

____

Kale & Strawberry Salad

Since Mrs. is on a health kick and kale is one of the "healthy" vegetables, she is always looking for ways to sneak it into our meals.

Ingredients and Directions:

- Start with one or two bunches of fresh kale. (If you don't know what kale is, ask your local supermarket produce person to point out the fresh kale.)
- Rinse well with cold water.
- Remove the kale leaves from their stems, chop the leaves into bite-size chunks, and place them into a large bowl.
- While buying the kale, grab some strawberries, too. Rinse and remove any leaves still attached. If not in season, frozen strawberries will do.
- Slice the strawberries onto the kale.
- Pour on some Lighthouse Strawberry and Poppy Seeds dressing (found at Publix) or your favorite dressing.
- Add some shaved almonds and toss together well.
- Next, add some chopped red onions and toss.
- Lastly, add fresh ground pepper and kosher salt. Do a final toss and chill well.
- Toss again before serving.

This is a simple salad with a flavor that makes a great impression on your guests.

Fish Recipes

Bob's Mahi Sliders

What do you do when relatives or visitors show up after you've caught, cleaned, and prepared the fish, and they are expecting to get some? One of our solutions is to make sliders.

Everybody has their own way of putting them together. It just so happens mine is one of the better ways.

Ingredients:

- ½ pound firm fish like Mahi Mahi or Snapper per 4 people; for more people, add more fish. (If you really like the person, then use 2 sliders per person. We like to use a baguette cut into ½-inch slices or dinner rolls to make things a little extra special, plus we use leftover baguettes with other recipes.)
- 1 shaker of Old Bay or your favorite seafood seasoning
- 4 tablespoons butter
- ½ cup of your favorite tartar sauce per 4 sliders. If you don't have a favorite sauce, a basic sauce recipe is provided below.
- Several leaves of lettuce
- Flour as per the requirement

Directions:

- Cut your fish fillets into ½-inch thick slices. Shape the slices to fit your baguettes with a little bit extra around the edges to make it look like you're not so stingy with your fish.
- Season each slice generously with our wonderful seafood seasoning and dredge in flour.
- Melt the butter over medium-high heat and fry your fish.
- To assemble, place a lettuce leaf on both sides of your lightly toasted baguette slices. Carefully place a fish slice on one side of the baguette and top the fish with a teaspoon of your tartar sauce. An option is to leave out the tartar sauce.
- We like to serve the sliders with an icy beer or a white wine.
- If tartar sauce is desired, see the recipe.

Tartar Sauce

Ingredients:

- ½ cup mayonnaise, *not salad dressing*
- 2 tablespoons finely chopped pickles (either sweet or dill pickles, according to preference)
- 1 tablespoon rice wine vinegar
- 1 tablespoon drained capers
- 1 teaspoon coarse-grained mustard
- About a pinch each of salt and pepper

Directions:

- Throw everything into a bowl, mix well, and cover.
- Cool down the sauce for 10 minutes to let the ingredients combine, then assemble your sliders.

Note: You may wish to adjust the various ingredients in the tartar sauce to suit your taste. Remember, the cook defines what tastes good. Since some people don't understand that rule, a skull fracture up the side of the head may be needed to help them learn.

Notes: _______________________________

____

____

____

____

____

____

____

Elaine's Sole with Vegetables

Every so often, Iron Skillet Elaine starts on this healthy kick and says you gotta eat more vegetables. I keep trying to tell her that fish with wine or beer is a healthy meal. Her comments really should not be included in the writing about that philosophy. So, in deference to Iron Skillet, here is a meal with vegetables in it. I still get to have my fish, wine, and beer, so we are both happy.

Ingredients:

- 2 tablespoons of butter
- 1 large onion, diced
- 1 cup cabbage, shredded
- 1 leek (the white and light green part) thinly sliced
- 1 large carrot, thinly sliced
- 1 large stalk of celery, thinly sliced
- 2 tablespoons water
- 2 pounds of sole or any whitefish fillets
- ½ teaspoon sea salt

For the Sauce

- ¼ cup sour cream
- 2 tablespoons butter
- 2 tablespoons flour
- ½ teaspoon salt
- ¼ teaspoon black pepper
- 1 cup chicken or fish stock

Directions:

- Sprinkle the fish fillets with salt.
- Melt the butter in a Dutch oven or skillet, add the vegetables, and stir-fry for 5 minutes.
- Place the fillets on the vegetables. Add 1 cup of water; cover and simmer for 15 minutes.
- To prepare the sauce, melt the butter in a saucepan, stir in the flour, and cook until golden brown (constantly stir the flour-butter mixture).
- Once the flour mixture is golden brown, gradually stir in the broth. (A whisk works better.)
- Continue stirring until the sauce boils.
- Transfer the sauce to the vegetable mixture and stir well.
- Transfer the fish to a warm platter.
- Season the veggies with salt and pepper; stir in sour cream.
- Pour the mixture over the fish on the platter.

Notes: ____

____

____

____

____

Fish Tacos

In getting ready for the Super Bowl, my wife and I like to prepare something that's easy and can be prepared in large or small quantities. In Southern California and Mexico, Fish Tacos fill that need. Here is our recipe for fish tacos.

Ingredients:

- 1-2 pounds of Grouper or other firm white fish
- 8 or more small (6-inch) flour tortillas (If you want to make them yourself rather than buy them, contact Iron Pot Bob at ironpotbob@eee.org for the recipe, or you can check online.)
- 3 cloves garlic, chopped
- 1 cup packed cilantro leaves
- 2 limes, zested
- 2 teaspoons ground cumin
- 1 ½ teaspoons salt
- 1 teaspoon black pepper
- ¼ cup tequila
- Here, we can try different methods of cooking fish. If you want to fry them, use a *fish batter mix* or make your own favorite and fry in oil at around 375°F. Or you can grill or smoke them.

Directions:

- Put all of the above ingredients except the tequila into a small blender for about 10 seconds.
- Add the tequila while the processor is running for another 15 seconds.

- Pour the above mixture into one of those Ziploc bags.

- Add the fish to the bag and store it at room temperature for 15 to 20 minutes, and ensure all pieces of the fish are evenly coated.

- Preheat your grill to medium-high. After cleaning your grates, rub them down with an oiled rag or use a grill cooking spray.

- Cook your fish until just cooked through, usually 3 or 4 minutes per side. Test with a fork to see if the fish flakes to the touch and is done.

- Smoking will take longer, but it is worth it. Just follow the directions for your smoker.

- If you are frying your fish, cut it into 2½ to 3½ inch strips long and ¾ inch wide. For a thicker coating, dip into a little flour, then into a lightly beaten egg mixture, and finally into your favorite batter mix. Otherwise, just coat it with your favorite frying mix.

- You can cook the fish in hot oil (around 375°F) until done. Try not to overload your fryer, as a lot of ingredients at one time can cause the oil to drop in temperature, and it can take longer to heat up to frying temperature. This results in an oily taste in your fish.

- Meanwhile, you will need some sort of coleslaw for your taco. Here's a version that we use:

Coleslaw

Ingredients:

- 2 cups shredded cabbage (You can use a combination of red and white cabbage, or NAPA cabbage works well, too.)
- 1 cup assorted baby greens such as baby spinach and butter lettuce, shredded (it's optional)
- 2 tablespoons tarragon vinegar
- 2 heaping tablespoons of sour cream
- Juice from 1 small lemon
- 6 green onions, finely chopped
- ½ teaspoon salt
- 2½ teaspoons sugar (After taste testing, you can add more sugar, but do so in small increments of ¼ teaspoon at a time.)
- 2 fresh limes cut into wedges

Directions:

- Combine the cabbage and greens in a bowl.
- Then combine the sauce ingredients, except the limes, in a small bowl.
- Pour ½ of the mixture over the greens and mix well.
- Heat your tortillas either in the microwave or on the griddle.
- Place one or two pieces of fish in the middle of the heated tortillas.
- Fold to create a pocket, and put at least 2 tablespoons of your coleslaw into the pocket.
- Squeeze a little lime juice on top of the slaw just before eating. Taste and add the extra dressing or more lime juice, if desired.

- Of course, one will need the appropriate beverages to accompany your tacos.

Notes: ____

____

____

____

____

____

____

____

____

Lox and Bagels

Way back in January 2017, Iron Skillet and I introduced something called Lox and Bagels. Since then, some of you have asked us how to make them. Here's the recipe for a two-person serving.

Ingredients:

- 2 to 3 mini-bagels per person
- 3 or 4-ounce package of lox (thinly sliced smoked salmon) per 2 adults
- 1 tub of whipped cream cheese (whipped is easier to spread) or 1-8 oz. A brick of cream cheese.
- 1 medium onion, thinly sliced
- 1 lemon cut into thin, squeezable slices
- 1 small jar of capers (optional)

Directions:

- Separate the mini bagels into the top and bottom halves and lightly toast.
- Spread a generous layer of cream cheese on each toasted bagel half.
- Drain a couple of tablespoons of capers if desired.
- If using capers, sprinkle some drained capers on top of the cream cheese.
- Carefully open the package of lox.
- Carefully separate the slices of lox using a sharp, thin knife and place one slice of lox covering the top of each cream cheese-covered bagel.

- Serve 3 or 4 halves per person with a pile of sliced onions and some lemon on the side for toppings, if desired.

Note: Experiment with and without onion on a bagel and squeeze a little lemon juice on top. Another popular variation is to add a fresh tomato slice to each bagel prior to serving.

Mrs. and I like this meal as breakfast with a strong coffee. We also like to pair it with some seasonal fruit.

To make this a special dish, consider the following wine: Lindeman's Bin 99 Pinot Noir 2014 (Australian). Described as a delicate style with bright cherry fruit and a hint of spice.

Notes: ____

____

____

____

____

____

Pan-Roasted Cod and Potatoes

Many times, folks have asked us how we come up with those wonderful recipes we share with you all. The answer is simple. *Everywhere*. When you have been around as long as the missus and I have been and like seafood as much as we do, and if it's really good, it doesn't matter the source. You just want to know how it's prepared.

We take the recipe and then tweak it to our tastes to make it wonderful. These are the recipes we share. We do have some traditional makings that we use. For example, in fish soups, stews, and ceviche, we try to sneak in the "royal three," onion, green pepper, and celery, in deference to our Cajun upbringing. When it calls for a hot pepper, we like to use datils, which are 100,000 to 300,000 on the Scoville scale. Tabasco is only 30,000 to 80,000 on the same HOTNESS scale. We discovered datil peppers while researching Minorcan cooking in St. Augustine, Florida. In fact, we liked them so well that we obtained several plants so we could save driving to St. Augustine when we needed more datils. We also spend a lot of time cooking with cast iron utensils, hence our monikers of "Iron Pot Bob and Iron Skillet Elaine." This next dish reflects the one-pot meal philosophy of many cast iron aficionados.

Since most of you don't regularly cook over a campfire, you'll have to use your oven and a large 12-inch cast-iron or equivalent frying pan. Set your oven to 450°, and let's get started.

Ingredients:

- 1 ½ pounds russet potatoes, peeled and sliced ⅛-inch thick
- 4 (6-8 oz.) skinless cod fillets at least 1 inch thick

- 4 tablespoons olive oil
- Sea salt and fresh ground pepper

Directions:

- Rinse the cut potatoes in cold water and pat dry.
- In a large bowl, toss the potatoes with 2 tablespoons of oil, 1 teaspoon of salt, and ¼ teaspoon of pepper, making sure the potatoes are evenly coated.
- You can use the remaining olive oil to coat the frying pan or spray on a release compound like PAM.
- Spread the potato slices evenly along the bottom of the frying pan.
- Cook the potatoes on medium-high heat until they turn kind of translucent around their edges. This usually takes about five minutes.
- Now that you have heated the pan and the potatoes, move the pan to the oven for about 15 minutes or until the potatoes are tender and starting to brown.
- Now season your cod fillets with salt and pepper and place skin side down on the potatoes.
- Put the skillet back into the oven and bake for about 15 minutes or until the potatoes are done and the fish flakes apart when gently prodded with a paring knife. If you want to test the fish with a kitchen thermometer, the fish should be at least 140°F.
- Slide a spatula under the potatoes and fish and transfer to individual plates.
- One serving suggestion is to make an orange salad to serve with your meal. You can use a couple of Florida oranges. Remove the skin and pith (the white part under the skin), then chop up the oranges and mix

with ½ cup parsley, 1 minced shallot, and 2 tablespoons rinsed capers. Add in a couple of tablespoons of red wine vinegar, a tablespoon of olive oil, then salt and pepper to taste. Serve this with the fish.

- If you want to spice it up, you might use a spoonful or two of your favorite salsas on the fish. Otherwise, just having some cut lemon available works well, too.

Notes: ____

____

____

____

____

____

____

____

____

Salmon with Cherry Tomato Salsa

Sometimes, with all the different fish available here in Florida, one can forget that there are other fish around the world, especially in foreign countries like Alaska and the western United States.

Sometimes, you can get confused because the same name can be used for different fish in different parts of the country. For example, the word "dolphin" in Florida is synonymous with Mahi Mahi. The word "dolphin" on the West Coast usually means the bottlenose dolphin or Flipper from the popular TV show of the last century. However, salmon still means salmon on both coasts. So, this recipe is a "salmon" recipe.

Ingredients:

- 4 salmon fillets, 4-5 oz. each
- 3 tablespoons olive oil, divided
- sea salt and pepper
- 1 large clove of garlic, minced
- 2 green onions chopped
- pinch of red pepper flakes
- 1 pint cherry tomatoes, quartered
- 2 teaspoons capers, rinsed
- 2 teaspoons red wine vinegar
- 2 leaves of fresh basil, chopped

Directions:

- To make the salsa, heat a skillet to medium and throw in the garlic, green onions, and red pepper flakes with a tablespoon of olive oil.
- Cook for about 4 or 5 minutes, then add the tomatoes and capers.
- Cook further for 10 minutes or until the tomatoes begin to soften.
- Meanwhile, preheat the oven to broil and line a cookie sheet with tin foil.
- Brush the salmon fillets with oil on both sides and place skin side down on the cookie sheet. Season the tops with salt and pepper.
- When the oven has heated up, place the salmon fillets in for about 4 minutes.
- Now add the red wine vinegar and half of the chopped basil to the salsa in the frying pan.
- Test the salmon. It should be flaking to your touch. If so, remove from the oven and plate with a heaping spoonful of salsa on top.
- Sprinkle the rest of the basil on top of the fillets to add color and make everything look good.

Notes: ____

____

____

Herb Roasted Orange Salmon

It seems that a lot of folks from the West Coast only know 2 fish, salmon and trout, even though Florida has over 26 different varieties of wonderfully edible seafood.

Mrs. and I thought we would at least give those poor folks a recipe for salmon to hold them over while educating them about Florida fish, shellfish, shrimp, and lobsters.

Ingredients:

- 2 tablespoons olive oil
- ¼ cup fresh Florida orange juice
- Finely grated zest of 1 orange
- 2 teaspoons minced fresh garlic
- 2 teaspoons dried tarragon
- 2 teaspoons fresh chives, chopped
- 4 salmon steaks (8 oz.)

Note: You can also use other fish, such as Grouper or Shark.

Directions:

- Mix together olive oil, orange juice, orange zest, garlic, tarragon, salt, and pepper.
- Add the mixture to a Ziploc-type bag along with the salmon.

- During the next hour, at room temperature, toss the salmon around once or twice.
- Meanwhile, preheat your oven to 475°F.
- Spray a baking dish with some sort of anti-stick spray.
- Bake the salmon for 7 or 8 minutes until the fish flakes easily when tested with a fork.
- Mrs. likes to serve each fish steak on its own bed of saffron rice. She likes to sneak in some sort of vegetable, but that's your choice.
- Serve with fresh baguettes and something cold to drink.
- Now, try this recipe with some fresh Florida fish and see what you have been missing.

Notes: ____

____

____

____

____

____

Red Snapper Yucatan Style

This is one of those recipes that we discovered quite by accident when we visited San Felipe, Mexico. It uses cumin, which was a strange spice to us at that time. You may want to approach the cumin a little at a time if you are not familiar with it.

Ingredients:

- 2 small chopped green peppers
- 1 medium onion, chopped
- 2 cloves garlic, finely chopped
- 4 tablespoons butter
- 2 tablespoons chopped coriander leaves or 1 teaspoon dried leaves.
- 1 teaspoon cumin
- ½ teaspoon grated orange rind
- ½ cup fresh orange juice
- 4 pounds Red Snapper, whole & cleaned
- 3-4 tablespoons sliced black olives
- 1 avocado, for garnish

Directions:

- Fry the first 3 ingredients in ½ the butter until softened.
- Add the coriander, cumin, orange rind, and orange juice; season with salt and pepper to taste.
- Simmer for 2 minutes.

- Coat the bottom of a Dutch oven with the rest of the butter.
- Place the fish in the pan, then pour the sauce over the fish and scatter sliced olives over the top of the fish.
- Cover and bake at 350°F for about 30 minutes, basting occasionally with the sauce. Hint: If using cast iron, heat it up a bit in the oven before you add the ingredients.
- Serve hot after garnishing with thin slices of avocado.

Notes: ____

____

____

____

____

____

____

____

____

Whole Grilled Snapper on the Hot Side

For you folks who like things on the hotter side, here is one of my "hotter" recipes. This recipe uses a Caribbean version of Scotch Bonnet called Ghost Peppers.

Here's to give you some idea of how the hotness in peppers is measured: the pepper industry uses Scoville Heat Units (SHU). The range can go from a Tabasco or Cayenne pepper at 30,000. Datil pepper at 100,000 to a Carolina Reaper at 1,570,000 SHUs. Scotch Bonnet and Habanero peppers start at 150,000 SHUs. These are the low ranges of these peppers. The high-end heat that these peppers can produce is almost double the low-end.

For you folks who don't like a lot of reading, all this means is that this pepper seasoning is very hot to a person's taste buds.

Ingredients:

- 1 whole Snapper, Pompano, or other 4-5 pound fish, cleaned but leave the head and tail on
- 3 Ghost peppers, Scotch Bonnet chilies, or Habanero chilies
- 4 juicy limes (1 will be thinly sliced, 1 will be halved, 1 will be squeezed, and 1 will be used as garnish slices)
- sea salt and freshly ground pepper
- 1 piece of ginger, 2 inches long, that has been peeled and cut into thin slices
- 2 cloves of garlic, thinly sliced

Directions:

- Rinse the fish in cold water, inside and out, drain, and dry with paper towels.

- Make 4 or 5 deep cuts, equally spaced on both sides of the fish.

- At this time, prepare the 4 limes according to the description in the ingredients list.

- Thinly slice two of the chilies. (You really should wear food-handling gloves when working with these chilies.)

- Rub the fish on both sides with the 2 halves of lime.

- Cut the third chili in half lengthwise and rub all over both sides of the fish.

- At this point, I like to use a mixture of sea salt and pepper to sprinkle in the cavity and into the deep cuts on each side of the fish.

- Now place one slice of each lime, chili, ginger, and garlic in each slit and under each gill. Stuff inside the cavity with any leftover seasoning.

- Place your fish on a large platter. Then, pour the juice from the squeezed lime over the fish and sprinkle salt and pepper over the entire fish.

- Cover and let it marinate in the refrigerator for at least 30 minutes.

- In cooking, you can grill your fish using the indirect method. (The food isn't placed directly over the flame but is placed off to one side of the heat source. You will want to preheat the grill to high.) Or if you use an oven, preheat it to 400°F.

- At this point, transfer the fish from the platter to a foil pan and pour any remaining juices from the platter over the fish. Place the pan in the oven or on the grill and close the grill.

- Cook the fish either way for 12 to 15 minutes per pound. Test by pressing on the flesh. If done, the fish will break into flakes.
- Transfer the cooked fish to a clean platter.
- If you want to show off, fillet the fish at the table by simply peeling the skin off the top of the fish using a fork and spoon. Then, using the side of the spoon, make a lengthwise cut down the back of the fish just above the backbone. Gently ease the spoon into the cut, loosening the fish from the bones along the entire side of the fish frame. Now, lift this beautiful fillet onto your platter if you have room. You should now be able to lift the head and backbone off the bottom fillet along with the tail. Next, turn this remaining fillet over to peel off and discard the skin.
- Place the 2 fillets on your serving platter, decorated with some lime slices, and wow your guests by allowing them to have a piece of this wonderful fish you have prepared.

We like to serve this on coconut rice, although any long-grain rice will do. If you have any seafood broth, you may want to cook your rice by diluting it half-and-half with water.

P.S. The chilies tend to lose a lot of their heat during cooking.

Notes: ____

____

____

____

Shrimp Recipes

Shrimp is the most common seafood eaten in the world. They are usually plentiful and can be prepared in a myriad of ways. Here are some of the recipes we found most popular over the years.

Bob's Redneck Shrimp

There's a time in every fisherman's life when they want to get the food from the water to their plate in the shortest amount of time possible. This month, I'm going to share with you one of our family's secrets on how to do it with shrimp. It's called Bob's Redneck Shrimp.

Ingredients:

- 1 lb. raw shrimp in any form, either head-on or head-off, but peeled and deveined
- 6 tablespoons of butter
- 3 heaping tablespoons of Old Bay seasoning

Directions:

- Melt the butter in a heavy frying pan over medium heat.
- After the butter is melted, mix in the Old Bay seasoning.
- Throw your shrimp in the pan, making sure they are evenly distributed. If necessary, cook in batches so that you don't overload the pan.

- Keep this shrimp moving in the butter sauce either by pan flipping or with a spatula or spoon. It should only take 2 or 3 minutes per side to cook. Of course, one will periodically have to ensure quality by careful periodic sampling, if you know what I mean.
- Turn off the fire and let the shrimp rest in the sauce for a couple of minutes while you get something to drink.
- Portion out the shrimp in bowls and spoon a little sauce on top. If you want to make the shrimp spicier, then sprinkle some additional Old Bay seasoning on the shrimp.
- Serve with lots of napkins and have some crusty French bread on the side so you all can soak up the butter sauce.
- Ice-cold beer goes very well with this recipe.

Note: Iron Skillet and I have used this basic sauce and cooking technique for a few years on many kinds of fish and meat when we can't wait to cook the food in some fancy way.

Notes: ____

____

____

____

Bacon & Ranch Shrimp Quesadilla

Since we are getting some good runs with shrimp, everybody wants to work with the big, bigger, and biggest shrimp and not waste a lot of time preparing the small ones, sometimes called cocktail shrimp. This recipe allows y'all to use some of the small ones, plus incorporate another Southern favorite: bacon.

For those of you who live in a culinary desert, a quesadilla is just a flour tortilla filled with goodies. Tortillas are becoming increasingly popular because you can treat them like a sandwich. Another derivative is a burrito, a flour tortilla filled with goodies and then wrapped or folded up. One advantage of a burrito is that it can be prepared ahead of time and carried with you when you go fishing. It can also be less messy to eat than a quesadilla or taco.

Ingredients for 2 quesadillas:

- ½ cup small peeled and deveined shrimp (or more if desired)
- 4 strips of bacon fried to a soft, crisp stage, cut or chopped into small pieces (pre-packaged or pre-fried bacon can be used)
- 4 flour tortillas of 8-inch
- 2 tablespoons of washed and chopped green or red bell peppers or other peppers to taste
- 1 tablespoon onion – sweet onion or green onion
- ⅓ cup of a good melting cheese to taste – Cheddar, Colby, or Monterey Jack is recommended

Shrimp seasoning:

- 1 teaspoon dried parsley

- ½ teaspoon garlic powder
- ¾ teaspoon ground black pepper
- ¼ teaspoon onion powder
- ⅛ teaspoon thyme
- 1 teaspoon seasoned salt
- 1 tablespoon lime juice

Tortilla seasoning:

- ½ teaspoon seasoned salt
- ½ teaspoon paprika (optional)
- ¼ teaspoon cumin (optional)
- 3 tablespoons canola oil

Directions:

For Spicy Ranch Dip:

- Take ½ cup sour cream. Light sour cream or plain Greek yogurt could also be used.
- Make a second blend of the first 5 "Shrimp seasonings" without the salt and lime juice this time.

Note: Whenever using dried herbs instead of fresh ones, rub the seasonings in the palms of your hands to "wake up the flavors."

- Add 2-3 drops of a cayenne pepper sauce, Tabasco, Frank's, Sriracha, or a sauce of your preference (can be omitted if you do not like much spice)

- ¼ teaspoon of paprika or chili powder
- Mix this Spicy Ranch Dip and refrigerate for at least 1-2 hours or overnight (or while recovering from a good night of shrimping!)

For Quesadilla:

- Mix fresh seasonings together or, if using dry seasonings, rub seasonings in the palms of your hands to "wake up the flavors."
- Mix lime juice and ½ of the shrimp seasonings.
- Drizzle the mix over peeled shrimp and marinate for at least one hour, tossing or stirring periodically.
- ¼ cup of shrimp stock can be substituted for the lime juice if a stronger shrimp flavor is desired. Discard the marinade before proceeding.
- Heat 1 tablespoon of canola oil to a medium temperature in a medium-sized frying pan about 8 inches in diameter.
- Sauté marinated shrimp for no more than 3 minutes. Stir occasionally as they cook.
- Remove the shrimp and place them on a paper towel-lined plate.

Note: If you use precooked bacon, add the bacon to the shrimp and sauté together.

- On a small plate, assemble the quesadilla. First, place one of the tortillas on the plate. Next, make sure to place some (more than ½ of the half of ⅓ cup) cheese reserved for each quesadilla on the tortilla. Place pieces of shrimp, bacon, onion, and peppers on the tortilla and spread evenly to have the same great flavor in each bite.

- Next, spread half of the remaining shrimp seasoning (no lime juice) on this tortilla, followed by the remaining half of the cheese reserved for the quesadilla.

Please note that you can also perform this step when the first tortilla is in the frying pan; however, you will need to hurry and use additional care not to burn yourself. If your frying pan can handle it, you can always just place the pan with the tortilla under your oven broiler (or in your barbecue and close the lid). Be careful not to burn the tortilla.

- In the same pan, prepare to heat another tablespoon of canola oil.
- When the oil starts to ripple (around 325°F), it is ready. Carefully place or slide a dry flour tortilla and its topping into the hot oil. If there is moisture under the tortilla, it may cause the oil to splatter. Quickly adjust any items that may have shifted, and then place the second tortilla on top. Begin to periodically check how the tortilla is frying after a minute and a half.
- The quesadilla is ready to flip when the first tortilla is a crispy, light golden brown. Carefully flip the quesadilla so as not to lose the ingredients. The cheese will help "glue" the items together if they have begun to melt together.
- Once the quesadilla has been flipped, quickly sprinkle on top any tortilla seasonings you may wish to use. You could use the ones specified here or use more of the ranch seasonings to bring out more of the flavor, especially if you do not like the spice of paprika, chili, or cayenne.
- When the second tortilla is light golden brown, simply slide the quesadilla onto a plate and use a pizza cutter to cut the quesadilla.

- Serve with spicy ranch dip. You could also serve it with guacamole, salsa, bacon ranch dressing, sliced black olives, chopped onion, or some fresh chopped tomato, jalapenos, etc. Use your imagination and have fun with this basic recipe.
- A few cooked shrimp can also be placed on top of the finished quesadilla for presentation or as an additional treat.

Notes: ____

____

____

____

____

____

____

Cajun Shrimp Bisque

When the weather starts getting cold here in Florida (that's when the temperature drops below 65°F), we start thinking about soups. This recipe was one we almost forgot about while waiting for the temperature to get below 65°. This is a shrimp soup or, if you want to get fancy, a Shrimp Bisque.

Ingredients:

- 3 tablespoons butter
- 1 onion, finely chopped
- 1 red bell pepper, seeded and finely chopped
- 2 sticks of celery, finely chopped
- 1 clove garlic, minced
- Pinch of dry mustard and pinch of cayenne pepper
- 2 teaspoons paprika
- 4 tablespoons flour
- 3 cups fish stock
- 1 cup heavy cream
- 1 sprig thyme
- 1 bay leaf
- 8 ounces raw, peeled, and deveined shrimp
- Sea salt and white pepper
- Snipped chives

Directions:

- Cut shrimp into ½ inch pieces, then place in a bowl and sprinkle with 1 tablespoon of Old Bay seasoning.
- Then melt the butter in a saucepan and add the onion, pepper, celery, and garlic.
- Cook until softened but not brown.
- Stir in the mustard, cayenne, paprika, and flour and cook for about 3 minutes over medium heat, stirring occasionally.
- Blend in the stock gradually until well blended.
- Next, add the thyme and bay leaf and bring to a boil.
- Add the cream and simmer for about 5 minutes or until thickened, stirring occasionally.
- Add the shrimp and cook until pink (about 5 minutes).
- Season with salt, pepper, and cayenne to taste.
- Serve in soup bowls.
- Garnish with the snipped chives.

Be sure to have lots of crusty bread on hand.

Notes: ____

____

____

____

____

____

____

____

____

____

____

____

Gazpacho Shrimp Cocktail

Iron Skillet, Elaine, and I gave a 'fish preparation demonstration' at the Halifax Sport Fishing Club a few years ago. Many folks seemed to want to make these recipes at home. This is one of four recipes presented at the show.

This recipe is called gazpacho and is a cold soup from Spain. Since we were presenting to a bunch of fishermen, we livened it up by adding shrimp, which made a wonderful cold soup for us to use any time.

Mrs. was happy because I finally came up with a recipe that had some vegetables in it. So here it is.

Ingredients:

- 1 small tomato, seeded and diced
- 1 small hot-house cucumber, peeled, seeded, and diced
- ½ green bell pepper, seeded and diced
- ¼ cup diced red onion
- ¼ cup chopped fresh cilantro
- 2 cups tomato juice; some cooks substitute plain V8 juice
- ⅓ cup red wine vinegar
- Juice of 2 limes (4 tablespoons)
- 1 teaspoon sugar
- 2 dashes of Worcestershire sauce
- 4 dashes of Tabasco sauce
- ¾ pound cooked, peeled, deveined medium shrimp (chopped into ½ inch to ¾ inch pieces)

Directions:

- Combine tomatoes, cucumber, green pepper, onion, and cilantro in a large bowl.
- Whisk together tomato juice, vinegar, lime juice, sugar, Worcestershire sauce, and Tabasco in another bowl. Pour over the chopped vegetables.
- Cut the shrimp into large ½ to ¾ inch chunks, add to the vegetable mixture, and mix well.
- Season with salt and pepper to taste.
- Cover with plastic wrap and chill for at least 2 hours.
- You can garnish with a celery stalk and a dollop of sour cream.

Have a bottle of your favorite hot sauce available for your guests to add for more heat. Notes: Suggested wine pairing: Belvino Pinot Grigio (Bardolino, Italy). This wine shows a balance of apple and pear fruit, with a touch of peaches on the middle of your palate and a hint of elderflower on the finish.

Notes: ____

____

____

____

Helen's Shrimp Corn Chowder

I was talking with Helen Klenk over at the fishing club the other day, and she was bragging about this bodacious Shrimp Corn Chowder recipe that she developed. I said, "The proof is in the eatin'. Lay it on me."

I tested it, and she is right. It is easy to fix and tastes great. Here it is.

Ingredients:

- 1½ or 2 pounds of shelled and deveined shrimp, cut into bite-size pieces
- 8 oz. package of cream cheese
- 1 medium onion, coarsely chopped
- 3 cans of cream of potato soup
- 1 can whole kernel corn (drained)
- 2¼ cups milk
- 2 teaspoons of Old Bay seasoning
- 2 cloves of garlic smashed
- ⅛ teaspoon cayenne pepper (you Florida crackers may want to increase this amount)
- 2 tablespoons butter
- Salt and pepper to taste

Directions:

- Sauté chopped onions, garlic, and shrimp in butter.
- Add the seasonings and melt the cream cheese into the sautéed mixture.

- Add the 3 cans of cream of potato soup, milk, and the drained corn—heat and test for seasonings. Remember, cayenne pepper is sneaky and can bite you really fast if you aren't careful.

P.S. Iron Skillet really likes this corn chowder.

Notes: ____

____

____

____

____

____

____

____

____

Hot, Avocado & Shrimp Soup

Iron Skillet Elaine wanted a quick soup recipe that would **WOW** our guests and relatives.

What makes this recipe "extra special" is the use of avocados. Avocado soup is a little tricky in that it is sensitive to overheating and will separate.

Ingredients:

- 1 small onion, finely chopped
- 2 stalks of celery, finely chopped
- 3-4 cups chicken broth
- 1 small bay leaf
- A pinch of mace
- 3-4 sprigs of parsley
- 2-3 avocados
- 1 cup peeled shrimp, cut into small bites

Directions:

- Throw the onion and celery into the chicken broth along with the bay leaf, mace, parsley, and a little salt and pepper seasoning.
- Simmer for about 15 minutes to give a good flavor to the stock.
- Strain the stock, return the liquid to the pot, and save the solids for later garnish.
- Peel and remove the seeds from the avocados and chop up the flesh.

- Put the avocados into your blender (everybody in Florida must have a blender to make margaritas and daiquiris) plus a little of the stock, then slowly add the rest of the stock.
- Put this mixture into the top of a double boiler pot and heat very slowly and gently. **Do not boil**. (If you don't have a double boiler, you can make one using a pot with a stainless steel bowl, making sure there is an air gap between the water in the pot and the bowl.)
- Next, add the shrimp to the mixture and cook slowly on low heat (180-200 degrees) until the shrimp is done.
- If you want to get really fancy, add a dollop of sour cream on top in the middle just before serving. Or, you can add a spoonful of the leftover strained veggies to the middle of the soup.
- Sprinkle with paprika and freshly chopped chives to make a beautiful presentation.
- We add either a pinch or two of cayenne or a pinch of chopped datil peppers to kick it up a notch. Each to their own taste.

Notes: ____

____

____

____

Shrimp Boil

I want to share one of my favorite shrimp meals. To start, get about ½ to ¾ pounds of shrimp for each of the men and about ¼ to ½ pound of shrimp for women and children. Of course, use Florida shrimp, not foreign farm-raised shrimp, unless you are desperate for shrimp.

If you can get deveined shrimp with the shells on, do so. Taking the shells off will give your friends something to do when their team is losing. Let's start with cooking the shrimp.

Ingredients:

- ½ cup of Old Bay seasoning; some prefer to use Zatarain's Crab Boil or make their own.

- 2 tablespoons of sea salt

- A rounded teaspoon of red pepper (cayenne)

- A whole sliced lemon or a couple of tablespoons of lemon juice

- 1 qt. water per person in a pot to cook shrimp

Directions:

- While that is heating up to a boil, I make my seafood sauce. The flavor of my secret sauce depends on the type of ketchup you use. You might have to experiment around to see what flavor you like best.

- I start with a cup of Hunt's Ketchup, then mix in a heaping forkful of prepared horseradish. And finally, I add up to a teaspoon of cayenne or red pepper.

As with all our recipes, you can change the quantities to suit your tastes, but keep in mind that cayenne is sneaky. It hits you when you think it's gone.

- After mixing, put the sauce in the refrigerator for at least 20 minutes so that the ingredients can become friends.

- When the water is boiling, throw the shrimp in until they are done, usually less than 5 minutes.

  I like to cheat and test one or two or three to make sure they're done, usually when they turn pink. You might want to keep an eye on the pot to make sure it doesn't boil over. Be careful not to overcook the shrimp. It tends to make them tougher.

- When the shrimp are done, drain and place the cooked shrimp in a bowl with a side of the sauce and some baguette bread (whatever that means; it's just a long skinny loaf of bread) and some really cold beer or wine.

After the game, the loser(s) have to do the cleanup and wash the pots and bowls. This last item makes for some really fierce cheering for their teams to win.

You really don't have to do this only for football. You can do this anywhere you have a pot, shrimp, spices, and something to drink.

Notes: ____

____

____

____

Shrimp Creole Appetizer

Many times, we have folks over but don't want to feed them a full meal, so we give them something called an appetizer, which means just a little bit. This shrimp recipe requires that you know they are coming over so you can prepare it ahead of time.

Ingredients:

- 4 cups shelled and deveined shrimp
- ¼ cup melted butter
- 1 garlic clove, crushed and finely chopped
- ⅛ teaspoon ground mace
- ⅛ teaspoon black pepper, or you can use cayenne instead
- Tabasco or your favorite hot sauce to taste
- Your favorite boil, like Old Bay or Zatarain's, to precook the shrimp

Directions:

- Cook the shrimp in your favorite Creole-type seasoning.
- Put shrimp, hot melted butter, garlic, mace, pepper, and Tabasco into your food processor or blender for about 10 seconds. You want to leave some texture in your mixture.
- If you want to get fancy, load up your pastry funnel with the mixture and squirt it onto Melba toast rounds or onto some small, freshly toasted pieces of bread.

We like to cut off the crusts and cut the toast in interesting shapes prior to toasting (less mess).

- Otherwise, pile the mixture into a small bowl or serving dish, throw some finely cut chives on top, stick a butter knife in it, and let the guests coat their own toast. If you don't want somebody like your brother-in-law to hog the whole thing, you can parcel it out into small dishes for everybody.

Note: This mixture can be kept overnight if covered and stored in the fridge.

This will go very well with a chilled white wine or an inexpensive champagne.

Notes: ____

____

____

____

____

Shrimp Cocktail

Serving a shrimp cocktail to your guests is one of the easiest appetizers around. Selecting shrimp for your cocktail can be as easy as buying precooked shrimp at the local grocery store or cooking your own.

We prefer to buy shrimp caught in the U.S., as it seems that many of the Asian imports may have been raised under questionable conditions. We like to get the raw 16 – 20 size; otherwise, any size will do if it is caught in the U.S.

Some people prefer the small cocktail or salad-type shrimp; however, keep in mind that the smaller the shrimp, the more peeling you have to do after cooking.

In terms of serving size, we like to use 4 ounces per serving for an appetizer. That works out to about five or six of the 16 – 20 size shrimp.

Ingredients:

- A box of your favorite crackers
- 4 oz. raw shrimp per person
- 2 oz. Old Bay seasoning or Zatarain's Seafood Seasoning per 3 qt. water
- 2 lettuce leaves per person
- 1 whole lemon cut into quarters per 4 persons
- 3 qt. water

Directions:

- Bring water to a boil and add Old Bay. If you want the shrimp to be spicier, add more cayenne pepper, ¼ teaspoon at a time.

- Add shrimp to boiling water and cook for 1 minute. Then turn off the heat.

- Let shrimp sit until firm and cooked through, about 2 or 3 minutes longer, depending on the size of the shrimp.

- Remove shrimp and let cool to room temperature.

- Remove shells and devein if necessary.

- Cool the shrimp in the refrigerator.

- Make the sauce while the shrimp is chilling.

For the Sauce

This is a remarkably simple cocktail sauce we developed to use on many things. Feel free to modify it to suit your tastes.

- Take ¼ cup catsup. Note that the catsup used will make a big difference in the final taste of your sauce. We use Hunt's Tomato Catsup.

- Mix the catsup with 1 tbsp. Horseradish. Note that the brand of horseradish you use will affect how strong the taste is. Find a taste you like and stick with that brand.

- Now, add ⅛ tsp. or less of Cayenne red pepper

- Mix all 3 together well, taste, and adjust.

- To let the flavor develop, cool the sauce in the refrigerator for 30 or more minutes and let the ingredients get to know each other.

- Keep in mind that the Cayenne and horseradish get more intense the longer they sit together.

Assembling

- Place sauce in small plastic sauce or butter cups.
  We usually find these in the picnic aisle of your local grocery store.

- Put 5 or 6 shrimp on the lettuce leaves along with two or three crackers.
- Serve along with several glasses of chilled white wine to add to the enjoyment of this appetizer.

Notes: _______________________________________

____

____

____

____

Shrimp Fajitas

Ingredients for 2 Fajitas:

- ½ cup of small to medium peeled and deveined shrimp (or more if desired)
- ½ cup washed and sliced green and/or red bell peppers.
- ½ cup sliced sweet onion (about ½ small onion)
- Your favorite Fajita seasoning (Chef Paul Prudhomme's Magic Seasoning Blends, Fajita Magic Southwest Flavor, McCormick Series, etc.)
- 2 teaspoons of lime or key lime juice
- 1 tablespoon butter
- 1 tablespoon Canola Oil
- 6-inch flour tortillas

Note: The amount of ingredients can be adjusted to your preference; a second seafood can be added if desired.

Directions:

- Mix the shrimp, ¾ teaspoon Fajita seasoning, and 1 teaspoon lime juice in a plastic bag or sealed container. Try to gently work the flavoring around all the shrimp.
- In another bag or container, mix the onion and peppers with ¾ teaspoon of the seasoning and 1 teaspoon of lime juice.
- Marinate in the refrigerator for about 2 hours, periodically gently mixing each bag.

- Prep the tortillas by dampening a paper towel with water and wrapping the flat 6-inch flour tortillas.

- Place in the microwave and pre-set for 20 seconds. DO NOT START YET. Please note that heating more than six tortillas at a time is not recommended. If you are heating more than two tortillas, add 5 seconds for each additional tortilla up to six, or a total of 40 seconds.

- Heat butter in a medium-sized frying pan over medium heat. When the butter turns a light brown, it is ready.

- Add the shrimp and slowly stir. After the shrimp have been coated with the butter and have begun to turn opaque on the edges (solid in appearance, not able to see through), about 30 seconds, add the tablespoon of canola oil, the peppers & onions, and 1½ teaspoons of Fajita seasoning.

- Toss and mix to allow shrimp to cook through (about 3 minutes). You want the vegetables to become tender but still crunchy. (The fancy word for slightly undercooked is "al dente.")
Note: If you prefer your vegetables to be tenderer or you do not want to use the butter, you can adjust the recipe.

- Just before pulling the pan from the heat, start the pre-programmed microwave to heat the tortillas. If you do more than one batch, adjust your process accordingly.

- Serve the tortillas on a warm paper towel or in a tortilla keeper.

- Serve the shrimp mixture directly from the pan into the warmed tortillas.

Optional flavored sour cream for serving:

- ¼ cup sour cream
- ⅓ scant teaspoon paprika
- ½ teaspoon Fajita seasoning

- Mix all the ingredients together well.
- Refrigerate for a minimum of 2 hours before serving.

Serving Suggestions: Serve with flavored sour cream, spicy ranch dressing, salsa, Pico de Gallo, guacamole, fresh chopped tomato, slices of lime, fresh chopped onion and peppers, coleslaw, etc.

Notes: ____

____

____

____

____

Stuffed Shrimp Plus

If you are looking for a different dish to serve special guests during football season, especially when FSU is playing, this shrimp recipe is the one to serve.

The nice thing about this dish is that we can prepare everything ahead of time and keep it in the refrigerator. Then, just finish cooking in the oven and serve during halftime.

Ingredients:

- 2 dozen raw shrimp, unpeeled (get the biggest shrimp you can)
- 4 tablespoons butter
- 1 small red bell pepper, seeded and finely chopped
- 2 green onions, finely chopped
- 1/2 teaspoon dry mustard
- 2 teaspoons dry Sherry (must be dry, not sweet)
- 1 teaspoon Worcestershire sauce
- 4 ounces of crab meat
- 6 tablespoons fresh bread crumbs
- 1 tablespoon chopped parsley
- 2 tablespoons mayonnaise
- 1 small egg, beaten
- Grated Parmesan cheese (grated, not powdered)
- Paprika, salt, and pepper

Directions:

- Shell and devein the shrimp.
- Butterfly the shrimp by cutting almost all the way through the curved side (where you deveined your shrimp), then press the shrimp open or flatten them.
- Melt ½ of the butter in a small pan and cook the pepper until softened (around 3 minutes).
- Then add the green onions and cook for another 2 minutes.
- Now add the rest of the ingredients: mustard, Sherry, Worcestershire sauce, crab meat, bread crumbs, parsley, and mayonnaise.
- Check the flavor and add any additional seasoning if necessary.
- Then, gradually add the beaten egg so that everything will stick together.
- Preheat your oven to 350°F.
- Place your flattened shrimp on a foil-lined cookie sheet and spoon the stuffing onto the shrimp.
- Sprinkle with the Parmesan cheese and paprika.
- Melt the remaining butter and drizzle a little bit over each shrimp.
- Bake for about 12 to 15 minutes or until the dressing is cooked through.
- Serve immediately.

Notes: ____

____

____

____

Lobsters and Crayfish

Oysters, Clams, and Mussels

This is the *love 'em* or *hate 'em* section. Some seafood fans think these are the best parts of seafood. Others think these are the bottom of the seafood barrel.

The missis and I fall into the first group. Here are some of our favorite recipes.

Boiled Crawfish

When we are having friends over, we like to treat them to something different. Most people are unfamiliar with crawfish, so we have a little fun with our foreign (Northerners) guests. We tell them that we are going to fix miniature lobsters just for them. But we are very careful not to say how miniature. You would be surprised at how short a time it takes for them to start to develop a taste for crawdads.

When we can, we like to use live crawfish that we get from several sources in Louisiana. We also like to get the largest crawfish that they have available at the time of our order. Our sources then FedEx them out, and we will have them the next day. If you don't want to wait for us to cook them for you, there are a multitude of crawfish festivals around most of the southern states and even in California. But here's our recipe for those who want to do it on their own.

Ingredients:

- 6 to 8 quarts of water
- 2 lemons, cut in half crosswise

- 4 medium-sized onions, quartered, with skins intact
- 2 celery stalks, including the leaves, cut into 3-inch lengths
- 1 dried hot red chili or 2 teaspoons red pepper flakes
- 4 garlic cloves, smashed
- 1 cup shellfish boil, such as Old Bay or Zatarain's, or you can make up your own boil using the enclosed recipe
- 2 tablespoons sea salt
- 20 pounds of crawfish, preferably live

Directions:

- Combine water, lemons, onions, celery, garlic, chili, shellfish boil, and salt in a 10-12 quart enamel pot and bring to a boil over high heat.
- Reduce heat to low and cover for 20 minutes.
- If using live crawfish, soak them in a large bucket of cold water for at least 10 minutes, then rinse them thoroughly in a colander set under cold running water. If using frozen crawfish, let thaw and then rinse thoroughly in cold running water.
- At the end of the 20-minute simmering time, bring the water up to a boil. Cook your crawfish in 5-pound batches, boiling them briskly at full boil, uncovered, for about five minutes. If using frozen crawfish, check one to make sure that it is cooked all the way through.
- Then, transfer the boiled crawfish to a heated platter, drop another 5 pounds into the pot, and cook those.
- Repeat the same procedure until all the crawfish are boiled.
- Then, serve them at once in their shells.

- At this point, you may have to show your guests how to eat your crawfish. Because they are so highly spiced, they are usually eaten without any accompaniment except our seafood sauce, cold beer, and maybe some crusty bread.

Note: In Louisiana, crabs and shrimp are boiled and served in the same way as crawfish. In the recipe above, you can substitute three dozen live blue crabs or 4 pounds of large shrimp in their shells, boiling them in one batch for 5 minutes. You can boil the crabs for 10 to 15 minutes in the same mixture.

Here is a recipe for your shellfish boil that can be used with crawfish, shrimp, or blue crabs. To make about 1 cup of seasoning mix, blend the following together in a jar and cover tightly. It can be stored in a dark place for up to 6 months.

Shellfish Boil Seasoning

- ¼ cup mustard seeds
- ¼ cup coriander seeds
- 2 tablespoons dill seeds
- 2 tablespoons whole allspice
- 1 tablespoon ground cloves
- 4 dried hot chilies or 1 tablespoon dried red peppers
- 3 medium-sized bay leaves finely crumbled

One trick we learned from some "old-timers" to increase the intensity of the taste, particularly for shrimp and crawfish, is that after they have cooked for about 5 minutes, turn off the heat and let everything sit in the boil for around 10 minutes.

Notes: ____

____

____

____

____

Clams with White Wine Sauce

Every so often, we score a bunch of clams at a reasonable price. Here's one recipe that we use with friends and sometimes relatives.

Ingredients:

- 4 dozen clams, well-scrubbed (we prefer little neck clams since they are a little more tender than their larger brothers and sisters)
- 1 cup cold water
- 4 teaspoons chopped shallots
- 2 teaspoons garlic, chopped
- 4 ounces of butter
- 1 cup dry white wine (We prefer a Chardonnay. Do not use sake or dry vermouth.)
- ¼ of a lemon
- 2 teaspoons chopped fresh parsley
- Freshly ground white pepper
- Plenty of French bread or baguettes cut into pieces for dipping in the sauce.

Directions:

- Steam the clams in the water until they open (approximately 5 to 10 minutes).
- Discard any clams that remain closed.
- Place the clams in a warm serving bowl and set aside.

- Reserve the cooking liquid for later use. You may want to strain the cooking liquid in case there's any sand at the bottom of the pot. (A coffee filter in a strainer works really well.)
- Sauté the shallots and garlic in 2 oz. of the butter for about five minutes, being careful not to allow them to brown.
- Stir in the reserved liquid and the white wine. Bring to a boil and simmer for about five minutes.
- Now, gradually add the remaining butter, but do not allow the sauce to boil.
- Season it with freshly ground white pepper and lemon juice. Stir in the chopped parsley and pour the sauce over the clams.

Note: Ensure enough liquid is in the individual bowls for dipping your freshly made garlic bread. We like to serve the clams in individual bowls with the sauce spread over the clams. Don't forget to have a large bowl handy to put the empty shells in. This goes well with the leftover chilled Chardonnay that you used for cooking.

Notes: ____

____

____

____

Crawfish Etouffee (Ay-To-Fay)

When most people think of Cajun, they think of jambalayas or gumbos. There is a similar dish called "etouffee." The difference is that etouffee, which means "smothered," starts with a roux, whereas jambalayas cook rice in the main dish.

Since Mrs. and I like crawfish, here is our crawfish etouffee recipe. Later on, I will give you a crawfish jambalaya recipe so you can compare.

Ingredients:

- 5 pounds of crawfish (live if available) or 2 pounds of crawfish meat
- 2 cups seafood stock
- 4 tablespoons brown roux; the recipe for roux is contained in the directions
- 1 cup finely chopped onions
- 1 cup finely chopped scallions, including 3 inches of green tops
- ½ cup finely chopped celery
- 1 teaspoon finely chopped garlic
- 1-pound can of tomatoes, drained and finely chopped
- 1 tablespoon Worcestershire sauce
- ¼ teaspoon ground red pepper (cayenne)
- 1 teaspoon ground black pepper
- 2 teaspoons salt
- 4 to 6 cups freshly cooked long-grain white rice

Directions:

- Begin by making a roux. You will need just these two ingredients: ½ cup vegetable oil and ½ cup all-purpose flour.
- Put the flour and oil into a Dutch oven or a large, heavy pot. Turn heat to medium-high, and cook, ***stirring constantly*** with a wooden spoon, until thick and bubbly, has a "peanutty" smell, and is dark brown, about 10 minutes. You must continuously stir the mixture or else it will burn, in which case you will need to start over.
- Set aside to cool and thicken.

The mixture is lava hot. Be very careful how you mix and handle it.

- Now, for the crawfish, if using live crawfish, soak them in cold water for at least 10 minutes, then wash them thoroughly under cold running water and drain.
- In a heavy 8-10 quart pot, bring 4 quarts of water to a boil over high heat. Drop them in the pot and boil them briskly for about five minutes.
- If using frozen crawfish, check one to make sure it is heated all the way through. If not, boil longer.
- If using only crawfish meat, drop the pieces into boiling water long enough to heat them up. Otherwise, you will have to get your crawfish meat by breaking off the tails and cracking out the meat, discarding the shells, heads, and other parts.
- Bring the fish stock to a boil in a small saucepan over high heat. Remove the pan from the heat and cover to keep it hot.
- In a heavy 5-6 quart casserole, warm the brown roux over low heat for two or three minutes, stirring constantly.

- Add the onions, scallions, celery, and garlic and cook over moderate heat, stirring frequently, for about five minutes or until the vegetables are soft.
- Stirring constantly, pour in the fish stock in a thin stream and cook over high heat until the mixture comes to a boil and thickens slightly.
- Add the tomatoes, Worcestershire sauce, red pepper, black pepper, and salt. Reduce the heat to low and simmer partially covered for 30 minutes.
- Then, stir in the crawfish meat and heat everything through.
- Now, taste and adjust the seasoning.
- Ladle the crawfish etouffee into a heated bowl alongside the rice in a separate bowl and serve at once.

Notes: We like to keep several different bottles of hot sauce on the table for those who want a hotter or spicier etouffee. Of course, you will need fresh bread to sop up any gravy that's left.

Notes: ____

____

____

____

Lobster – Cooking & Eating

When the lobster season is here, the Mrs. and I have started reviewing some of our ways to prepare lobster. First, you have the northeastern lobsters (the ones with the claws) or the spiny lobsters from Florida and California. Many folks say the spiny lobsters are slightly sweeter and tenderer than the northern or Yankee lobsters.

The basic ways to prepare your lobsters once you obtain them are to either BBQ, bake, broil, or boil them. Frying is generally not a good way to cook your lobster. Mrs. and I prefer to boil our lobsters. This method keeps them moist and tasty.

To boil your lobsters, you need a pot big enough to hold your lobsters. Next, fill the pot with enough water to cover your lobsters. We add about ¼ cup Old Bay seasoning. Some folks like to use Zatarains instead. We then add 1 teaspoon of sea salt per lobster and ⅛ teaspoon of cayenne per lobster. We also throw in some fresh lemon juice and bring everything to a boil. Next, add the lobster. It can be live or not live, but figure about 10 to 12 minutes of cooking time. To increase the impact of the seasoning, turn off the burner and let the lobsters sit for another 5 to 10 minutes. While the lobsters are cooking, melt some real butter and cut up your lemons. At this point, you may want to be running quality control on your adult beverage.

Now comes the fun part… eating your lobster. We prefer to use kitchen shears (not poultry shears) and small forks. If your lobster has claws, break off the claws from the main portion of the body. Next, break off the legs, and finally, remove the tail by breaking it off. There are several ways to remove the tail meat: You can cut it out with your kitchen shears by removing the soft membrane on the bottom of the tail, or you can break off the fan at the end of the tail and push your fork through that end, pushing the meat out. Now you have a luscious piece of meat that you can cut and eat or dip in butter, sprinkle a little lemon on, and enjoy.

This is where most people waste their lobster and crab. Separate the top caprice (the top part of the shell that covers the body) from the bottom by just pulling them apart. What you are now looking at will be the liver, which is an acquired taste for some folks. It may be covered with red eggs if the lobster is a female. Some people like those eggs also. Some people don't. You will also see some membrane-like material that is the lungs, which can be removed by simply scraping it off with your finger. What you have left is the portion of the lobster where its legs were attached. Each one of those legs has a muscle to move it. There is a thin membrane between each one of those muscles that you don't eat. Lastly, go for the legs and the meat in each segment. Here, the kitchen shears are handy for getting at the meat.

To balance out your lobster, we like to have a crusty baguette, some fresh Florida tomatoes, and several different kinds of adult beverages.

If you want to broil your lobster tails, cut out the membrane from the bottom, put them on a hot barbecue topside down, and brush the exposed meat with fresh butter. Cook for 5 to 7 minutes, turn over, and cook for 2 or 3 more minutes or until the meat is white all the way through.

Because of the heat of the barbecue, one will need an icy beverage to help the cook stay cool. Serve with a slice of baguette and a side of sliced tomatoes.

If by chance you should have leftover lobster, you can either give it to Iron Pot Bob and his Mrs. or use it to make a really nice lobster salad.

Notes: _______________________________

____

____

____

____

Minocran Clam Chowder

Mrs. and I have been on a 30-year search for THE clam chowder recipe. One day, while trying to find out what they were catching off the pier at Flagler Beach, Florida, we stopped in at the Funky Pelican restaurant. There was this weird name on the menu for a type of clam chowder. We tried it. It was very good.

We spent the next few months tracking down the secret Minorcan ingredients in this chowder. The Minorcan history is that indentured servants were brought to New Smyrna, Florida, and were treated more like slaves than indentured servants. Since they didn't like the working conditions, they left and went to St. Augustine, where they were protected by the governor there. Meanwhile, they brought their native cooking cuisine with them.

One of the basic ingredients is the datil pepper. While this pepper may have come from Cuba (some debate on the origin), it appears the only place in the whole world you can get them, even though they can grow almost anywhere, is in St. Augustine. And only at certain times!

In October, the people in St. Augustine have a Datil Festival, where each restaurant has samples of their version of Minorcan chowder. These little yellow peppers rank in hotness with the habanero peppers but have a sweeter, fruitier flavor.

Start off slowly when adding them to the mixture, and wear gloves (and safety goggles) when handling them. Also, keep in mind that there are as many Minorcan clam chowder recipes as there are clams. The following recipe is one that we like.

Ingredients:

- First, you have to get at least 2 pounds of clams. We use the little neck clams because they're usually easiest to find in the stores.
- 2 ounces of smoked bacon or 2 ounces of salt pork, chopped up fine
- 1 tablespoon of olive oil or coconut oil
- 2 teaspoons of thyme, dried or fresh
- ½ teaspoon dried marjoram
- ½ teaspoon dried oregano
- 3 cloves of garlic, chopped fine
- 1 bay leaf
- 1 green bell pepper, chopped into ¼ - ½ inch squares
- 1 (28-ounce can) of crushed tomatoes plus 2 or 3 fresh tomatoes chopped
- 1 large yellow onion, chopped into ¼ - ½ inch squares
- 3 small datil (¾ inch long) peppers
- 1 pound of your favorite potatoes, cut into ¼ - ½ inch squares
- 3 cups of seafood stock (you can buy this in your local supermarket, or you can make your own fish stock). See the appendix for stock recipes.

Directions:

- Now, let the fun begin.
- Rinse and clean your clams.
- Put 1-2 inches of water into a large pot. Bring the water to a boil and then drop in the clams. Cover and let steam for several minutes until the clams are all open.

- Remove the clams and put them in a bowl to cool down. Meanwhile, scoop out the water that you cooked the clams in and reserve it. Set aside a cup of the juice. Don't scrape the bottom of the pot, as there may be some leftover sand down there.

- When the clams are cool enough to handle, remove the clam meat from only the open ones.

- Discard the unopened clams along with the empty shells.

- Heat the oil in a large pot, then add the chopped bacon or salt pork. Cook until crisp (about 3 or 4 minutes).

- Combine all the spices, datil pepper, onion, and bell pepper in the pot with the bacon. You want to cook this mixture until the onion is golden brown. You will need to keep stirring every minute or two to prevent burning. Be careful here, as the oil from the pepper combines with the steam and will sting your eyes.

- Now add the seafood stock, 1 cup of your saved clam juice, and the tomatoes with juice, and bring it to a boil. If you don't have enough clam juice, add enough water to equal one cup of liquid.

- Reduce to medium heat. Add the potatoes and cook until they are tender.

- Throw in the clams when the potatoes are done, and heat up everything.

- Taste the chowder before adding sea salt and freshly ground pepper, as you may not need any.

- How many datil peppers you put in the chowder will determine how much cold adult beverage you will have to provide.

You should get about eight single servings from this recipe. When we make it, the Mrs. and I generally wind up eating about half of it while doing quality control testing. We like to serve this with a loaf of French bread and let each person tear off what they want. If you do it this way, encourage everybody to wash their hands first.

Notes: ____

____

____

____

____

Mussels with Tomatoes

Mussels are often misunderstood or confused with barnacles. Mussels are not barnacles; plus, many times, they are a bargain in your local stores. Today, Iron Pot was told by the Skillet. It's time to share some of your personal recipes, "or else (whatever that means). So, to keep everyone happy, I'll give up this one.

Ingredients:

- 2 pounds of fresh mussels.
- 2 cups of white wine (if there is any left after your quality control checks, chill it down to serve with the mussels, or just chill down another bottle)
- 1 can of 16-ounce size Italian-style chopped tomatoes
- ½ stick butter
- 1 teaspoon salt
- 4 cloves fresh garlic, roughly chopped
- ¼ cup fresh basil leaves, roughly chopped, loosely packed
- 2 shallots roughly chopped (You can use about ¼ cup fresh chopped green onions for milder onion flavor. Yes, you can use some of the green parts also.)

Directions:

- Rinse and scrub the mussels in cold water (just to get rid of any sand and most of the beard).

- Fill a large pot with at least 1 inch of water, add mussels, cover, and bring to a boil.
- Boil until the shells open in about five minutes.
- Throw out any mussels that didn't open.
- Add remaining ingredients and cook on medium-low (175°F) heat for about 15 minutes.
- We like to serve the mussels in large bowls with some of the juice. Try to evenly distribute the tomatoes and onions among the bowls to make them look pretty.
- You will also need crusty bread and a chilled white wine. Mrs. will sometimes serve a simple salad with a light dressing.

Notes: ____

____

____

____

____

Red Eye Oysters

I've been bugging my friend, Capt. Don Martin has been trying for almost a year now to get his prize-winning "Red Eye Oyster" recipe. After much begging and some serious horse-trading, he finally gave in. Here it is:

The first part is the hardest. You need about 24 shucked oysters. If you don't like to shuck them yourself and can't get someone else to shuck them for you, then here's a trick I use.

First, you get 24 same-size oyster shells and clean them really well. Then you get a couple of pints or a quart of shucked oysters. Sort the oysters out so that they all fit the shells you have. As for the rest of the oysters, you may want to run a quality control check or use them to make my Cajun Oyster Recipe.

Now for the wonderful part, get the following ingredients together before you start assembling.

Ingredients:

- ¼ cup butter
- ¼ pound blue cheese
- 1 large stalk of celery, finely chopped
- 1½ tablespoons Worcestershire sauce
- ⅓ cup sour cream
- ⅓ cup fresh bread crumbs
- 1 hard-boiled egg chopped
- ¼ teaspoon cayenne (red pepper)
- ¼ teaspoon liquid smoke

- Louisiana Hot Sauce (or similar)

Directions:

- Melt the butter in the top of a double boiler. If you don't have a double boiler, use one pot sitting on top of another pot of boiling water.
- Add cheese, celery, and liquid smoke to the pot. Get the cheese starting to melt, and then add the Worcestershire sauce, sour cream, bread crumbs, and pepper to taste. Combine well.
- Either preheat your oven to 375°F or prepare your coals on the grill. While everything is heating up, add approximately 1 tablespoon of the mixture on top of each oyster.
- Place the oysters in a pan if using the oven or on the grill if using the barbecue for approximately 8 to 10 minutes until the topping is bubbling and is a light golden brown.
- Bring the oysters out, put a drop of hot sauce on each one (the Red Eye), and serve them hot to your guests.
- If you want to get fancy, you can serve the oysters on a bed of rock salt with a glass of good Florida wine or another cold beverage.

The trouble with this recipe is that you run out of oysters before you run out of people wanting more. Many thanks to Capt. Don Martin.

Notes: ______________________________

____

____

____

____

Steamed Oysters in Garlic Butter Sauce

One of our favorite crustaceans is oysters. We usually like our oysters raw with Bob's Seafood Sauce, some lemon juice, and, of course, a hot sauce like Tabasco or hotter. Occasionally, we cook oysters by frying, steaming, BBQing, or the way described below.

Ingredients (per person):

- 6 to 8 oysters (shucked or in-shell)
- 1 to 2 tablespoons of real butter per oyster
- 1 clove garlic (smashed and finely chopped) per 3 oysters
- Pinch of cayenne pepper per 2–3 oysters (optional, for heat)
- Plain breadcrumbs (enough to cover each oyster)
- Optional: 1 teaspoon white wine per 2–3 oysters (for a fancier butter sauce)
- Crusty bread (like a baguette), for serving
- White wine or beer (chilled), for serving

Directions:

- If using oysters in the shell, shuck them and leave them in their shells.
- If using pre-shucked oysters, place 6 to 8 oysters per person in small oven-safe dishes.
- In a small pot over low to medium heat, melt 1–2 tablespoons of butter per oyster.
- Add finely chopped garlic (1 clove per 3 oysters) to the melted butter.

- Optional: Add a pinch of cayenne per 2–3 oysters for heat.

- Optional: For a fancier twist, add 1 teaspoon of white wine per 2–3 oysters.

- Set your oven to 400°F (200°C).

- Arrange oysters in their shells on a rimmed baking sheet or in prepared oven-safe dishes.

- Spoon a dollop of the melted butter and garlic sauce over each oyster.

- Sprinkle plain breadcrumbs over the top of each oyster.

- Place in the preheated oven.

- Bake until the breadcrumbs are golden brown.

- Remove from the oven and serve hot.

- Pair with crusty bread and a nicely chilled white wine or beer.

Notes: ____

____

____

____

Crab Recipes

Crab is another popular seafood. The most preferred, and the most expensive, is the Alaskan King Crab. However, there are many local crabs such as Blue Crab, Snow Crab, Stone Crab, and soft-shell crab, just to name a few. These crabs are smaller and require more effort to get to the meat, but are worth it. You can also find crab meat in cans.

B & E's Crab Delight (Appetizer, Dip, or Entrée)

Everybody has a "go-to" recipe that is pretty versatile in that it can be served as an appetizer or entrée, or even as a dip. We would like to share one of our "go-to" recipes with you.

We normally have all of the ingredients around the house to use in normal cooking. The most expensive item is either the crab or the shrimp. We just keep an eye out for when the cans of claw meat or chunk crab are on sale, and, depending on our resources, we will get one or two cans of crab meat to keep in the fridge for when y'all come over. The shrimp is easily purchased the same day we are going to use it, and, obviously, we use fresh Florida shrimp whenever it is available.

Enough talking. Let's cook!

Ingredients:

- 4 tablespoons butter
- 1 cup heavy cream or half-and-half
- 4 tablespoons flour

- 4 or 5 tablespoons dry Sherry
- ¾ cup grated sharp cheese
- 1 pound crabmeat or 1½ pounds chopped shrimp
- ⅛ to ¼ teaspoon cayenne

Directions:

- Melt the butter in a saucepan over medium-low heat.
- Gradually add the flour, stirring constantly to make a smooth paste.
- Cook for three minutes, then increase the heat to medium, gradually adding your cream while constantly stirring until the sauce is thickened.
- Remove from the heat and stir in the crab meat or shrimp.
- The type of dish you cook in this final step will depend on how fancy you want it to be. If this is your main dish (the fancy word is entrée), then put it all in one buttered dish/bowl.
- If serving as an appetizer, spread it out among 4 to 6 small, buttered dishes, putting no more than 5 or 6 ounces of mixture in each dish.
- For a hot dip, we like to put a heaping tablespoon in small individual dishes with crackers.
- Sprinkle the top of the mixture with the grated cheese and bake at 400°F for about 10 minutes or until the cheese melts and takes on a nice, light brown color. Be careful about overcooking.

Note:

1. As with any alcohol, be sure to run quality control checks, just in case.

2. This can be stored in the freezer, covered tightly with saran wrap, for several weeks and gently reheated in the microwave.

3. The leftovers are a great addition to your breakfast omelets.

Simply make your egg mixture using 3 eggs, 1 or 2 ounces of heavy cream, up to ¼ teaspoon of Cajun seasoning, and ⅛ teaspoon white pepper.

Mix well with a fork, then spread approximately ¼ cup of the egg mixture to cover the bottom of a small nonstick frying pan. Cook until almost done, and then spread 1 heaping teaspoon of your leftover crab mixture across one-half of your omelet and fold over the omelet. Heat until fully cooked.

Notes: ____

____

____

____

____

Crab Meat Quiche

Sometimes, when we know some very special friends or even relatives are coming over, Iron Skillet will go to the trouble of making a Crab Meat Quiche.

Most of the time, though, we just open a can of crabmeat and throw it into a bowl with mayonnaise and cayenne. Then let people dig in with whatever crackers are on sale that month.

Ingredients:

- 1 unbaked 9-inch pie shell
- 2 eggs
- 1 cup half-and-half
- ½ teaspoon salt
- Pinch of cayenne (ground red pepper) or more if you prefer a hotter taste
- ¾ cup (about 3 ounces) shredded Gruyère cheese
- 1 tablespoon flour
- 1 can (7½ ounces) crab meat, preferably Alaskan King crab, drained and flaked

Directions:

- Prick the bottom and sides of an unbaked flour pie shell.
- Bake at 450°F for 10 minutes until lightly browned.
- Beat together eggs, half-and-half, salt, and red pepper. Then combine with the cheese, flour, and crab.

- Gently spread the egg mixture into the cooked pie shell.
- Bake, uncovered, at 325° for about 45 minutes or until the tip of your knife inserted in the center comes out clean.
- Let cool down for 10 minutes, then cut into wedges and serve.

Note: how well you like your guest will determine how big the wedges are. You should get about 12-16 appetizers per 9-inch pie.

This should take about an hour from start to finish, assuming you have all the ingredients.

This is a nice brunch dish when served with a chilled white wine.

Notes: ____

____

____

____

Seafood Stews

Bob's Seafood Stew

What do you do with leftover fish and shrimp…? You make a seafood stew…!

This is an easy recipe, very mild, and reheats well. I suggest that you cut up, chop, and measure everything before you start cooking.

Ingredients:

- Start with about a pound or so of fish cut into 1-inch cubes. I like snapper or cod, or any other fish with firm flesh.
- Next, you need around ½ pound or more of Florida Shrimp.
- Now chop up a cup each of onion and green bell pepper.
- Chop ¼ cup of celery.
- As an aside note, the onion, green pepper, and celery are the "Royal Three" ingredients found in many Cajun recipes.
- 6 cloves garlic, minced
- 1 jalapeno pepper finely chopped (Remember to take the seeds out if you don't want it too hot.)
- To give it a bit of a Caribbean flavor, add ½ cup of unsweetened coconut milk.
- 1-14 ½ oz. can diced tomatoes
- ½ cup chopped cilantro plus 2 tablespoons extra for garnish
- 2 tablespoons of olive oil
- 1 tablespoon of fresh lime juice

- ½ teaspoon of salt
- ¼ teaspoon of white pepper or black pepper

Directions:

- The preparations are now complete. The cooking begins here. To start, put the fish in a Ziplock bag or bowl with a tablespoon of olive oil, lime juice, and salt and pepper. Make sure to coat the fish cubes with the mixture.
- In your soup pot, at least 3 quarts or larger, heat the remaining olive oil over medium-high heat and add the onion, green pepper, garlic, and jalapeno.
- Cook until the onion is tender.
- Then add the can of tomatoes (including the liquid) and the coconut milk. Heat to a boil. Add the cilantro, fish, and shrimp, heat to a boil, and then reduce to a simmer. Simmer until the fish flakes easily with a fork, about 5 or so minutes.
- I like to serve this on Louisiana long-grain rice. As with most rice (except minute-type rice), you may want to rinse the rice several times to remove most of the starch on the outside before cooking. And be sure of the cooking time for the rice, since it varies among different types of rice. A mild white wine goes well with this.

Notes: _______________________________________

____

____

____

____

Ceviche

Ingredients:

- 1-pound medium shrimp, peeled and deveined
- ½ pound of Bay scallops (that's those little ones)
- 4 ounces each of fresh lemon juice and lime juice
- 1 hothouse cucumber that is peeled and seeded, and chopped into ½ inch cubes or about the size of your Bay scallops.
- ½ cup of red onion, chopped very fine
- Up to ½ cup of finely chopped chilies, depending on your taste. I like to use Serrano chilies, but you can use your favorite hot chilies instead.
- 1 cup of seeded and diced fresh tomatoes
- If you want to go extra fancy, chop up an avocado into the same size cubes as your cucumber (about a half-inch cube).
- 1 tablespoon of fresh cilantro (or more if you want to make it hotter).

Note: The cilantro also makes a nice garnish if you're serving it to in-laws.

Directions:

- First, cut the shrimp into ½ inch chunks.
- Put the shrimp, scallops, cucumber, red onion, and chilies into a glass or stainless-steel bowl.
- Pour the citrus juices over everything and mix well. If more liquid is needed, add orange juice 1 ounce at a time.

- Let your mixture sit at room temperature for about ½ hour before chilling. (This lets the citrus juices "cook" the ingredients.)
- About an hour or so before you are ready to serve, remove the bowl from the refrigerator and add the tomatoes, avocado, and cilantro.
- Mix well and chill again.
- Just before serving, taste. You may or may not want to add salt and/or more cilantro, if necessary.
- This recipe should make about six servings.
- If you want to get fancy, chill whatever you're going to serve in and garnish with cilantro. Since this is a good hot weather dish, you will want to serve something cold to drink.

Note: The following wine was "officially" tasted and found to pair well with this recipe: Bellini Frascati 2015 (Rufina, Italy), described as crisp, with hints of tree fruit and floral notes.

Notes: ____

____

____

____

____

Seafood Paella

Every now and then, Mrs. wants to show off by having me cook a special seafood Paella. Now let me warn you that whoever you invite had better be worth it because this isn't an inexpensive meal.

Ingredients:

- 1 tablespoon butter
- 1 cup diced onion (we like to use red onion, but yellow onion will do)
- 1 cup long-grain white rice
- 1 medium green bell pepper, seeded and finely chopped
- 1 medium red bell pepper, seeded and finely chopped
- 1 tablespoon fresh minced garlic
- ½ teaspoon saffron threads, crumbled (You can sometimes find a less expensive Mexican saffron in the packaged spices section of the grocery store). If you don't see saffron on the shelf, ask the manager because it is so expensive that the store may keep it under lock and key.
- 2 ½ cups fish stock (Usually found in the chicken and beef broth section of the soup aisle in your grocery store). If you can't find the fish stock in the store, we have included some stock recipes in the index.
- 1 (6 to 8 ounce) lobster tail. Remove the meat from the shell and chop the meat into large pieces. Some seafood stores carry canned lobster meat if you're willing to pay for it.
- ½ pound king crab legs, shelled and chopped into large pieces
- ¾ pound flounder or other mild fish fillets, cut into large pieces

- ¼ pound raw sea scallops (These are the small ones or Bay scallops, not the large ocean scallops)
- ¼ pound large Florida shrimp, peeled and deveined
- ¼ pound of cooked clam meat
- ¼ pound each of squid and octopus, precooked and chopped into smaller pieces
- At this point, one might like to imbibe in something like Long Island iced tea to cool down after the shock of the bill for the above.

Directions:

- In a large (3 to 5 quart) stockpot, melt the butter and then sauté the onions on medium heat until softened (about 2 minutes).
- Then add salt and pepper to taste.
- Add the rice and stir for about 30 seconds. Do not brown the rice.
- Now add the bell peppers, garlic, saffron, and 2 cups of broth.
- Heat on medium-high until boiling, then lower to medium or lower and simmer for 10-15 minutes.
- Then add the seafood mix and remaining liquid.
- Cook uncovered for 15 to 20 minutes or until the rice is tender.

Note: Serve in bowls with chunks of crusty bread and a chilled adult beverage.

Notes: ______________________________

____

____

____

____

Slavic's Fish Stew

The other day I had the privilege of spending some quality time with Chef Slavic who is the executive chef from Down the Hatch Restaurant in Ponce Inlet, Florida.

Ingredients:

- 2 pounds of grouper
- One whole medium onion, chopped into ½- ¾ inch chunks
- 2 stalks of celery, chopped into ¼-inch bits
- Two 29-ounce cans of tomato sauce
- 10 ounces of chili sauce
- 2 ounces of Worcestershire sauce
- 1 ounce of Tabasco (be prepared to add more to hot'n to your taste)

Directions:

- Start with 2 cups of seafood broth (recipe included in the appendix if not found at the store). Be prepared to add more broth, if necessary, for taste and consistency.
- Begin by dusting the groper lightly with seasoned salt.
- Then steam your grouper pieces until they are done. Let cool. (I found that I like to use those bamboo steamers; they are fast and do a great job.)
- In a large pot, combine the onions and celery with a little coconut oil over medium-high heat until just softened.
- Add the rest of the ingredients and heat until just starting to boil.

- Now add the grouper (that you have previously chunked to bite-sized) to the mixture and simmer.

- After about 10 minutes of simmering... Taste.

- Adjust hotness by adding more Tabasco (½ ounce at a time) and/or more seafood broth.

- The wife and I experimented with adding some of our favorite wine to the mixture. However, if you choose to add other ingredients, put a ladle full into a separate bowl for mixing and tasting first. We also experimented with adding crab, but that didn't seem to go very well with the other ingredients.

- Serve in soup bowls and be sure to take from the bottom as the ingredients tend to settle out. Of course, you will have to serve your favorite adult beverage and a crusty baguette with this delightful dish.

Notes: ______________________________________

____

____

____

____

Desserts

Key Lime Dessert---Bachelor Style

It seems like a lot of you folks like my fishing recipes but are now asking for more, like dessert. For you rednecks out there, dessert is simple. Just open another cold can or bottle of your favorite beverage. For the rest of you, here's a bachelor-style (it's easy and cheap to make) key lime pie.

Ingredients:

- 2 Graham cracker pie crusts
- 1 pound of Key Limes or a small bottle of Key Lime Juice
- One 8-ounce softened brick of cream cheese
- 16 ounces of extra creamy Cool Whip
- 1 small can of Eagle Brand Condensed Milk

Directions:

- Piecrusts: You can make your own from scratch, or you can pick up a couple of ready-made graham cracker crusts in your local supermarket. You will need two pie crusts and the following:
- Key lime juice: 4 ounces (half a cup). There are two ways to get your key lime juice. You can go buy about a pound of key limes and squeeze them yourself. But unless you have an electric squeezer to squeeze the limes, your fingers will fall off (just joking). The other way is that you can get the store-bought key lime juice and use that. Now, there is a difference between the two juices. If you don't believe me, test it yourself using a teaspoon of each juice, being sure to drink a sip of

water before each taste. If you can't tell the difference, then save your fingers and use the store-bought key lime juice. If you want more pucker (like your first kiss), then increase the lime juice in the mix by adding 2 ounces more lime juice at a time.

- Now comes the hard part. In a bowl, place the softened cream cheese, Eagle Brand Condensed Milk, Cool Whip, and 4 ounces of lime juice. Mix until smooth. You MUST run the appropriate quality control on the mixture. Does it have enough tartness? If not, add more lime juice and taste again. Repeat if necessary until it tastes good to you. Then, you pour that mixture into the graham cracker pie crusts. Put your pies into your refrigerator, icebox, or cooler for at least an hour or two. Overnight is better.

- If you want to be really fancy because the company is coming over or to impress your girlfriend (remember, this is a bachelor's key lime pie), then sprinkle some very finely chopped or grated lime peeling (the green part only) on top. Just to make it look pretty. The peeling does add some extra zing to the taste.

- A variation on this is to pour the mixture into a chocolate cracker piecrust or put the mixture into individual little bowls and serve with those "ladyfinger cookies" (not ladyfish).

Hint: If you take longer than 15 minutes to make this, you have a problem. It takes my mother-in-law 17 minutes because she's 104 and doesn't see well.

Notes:

You can serve this with strong chicory coffee or a very cold white wine.

Bob's One-a-Day Chocolate Chip Cookies

Ingredients:

- ½ pound butter, softened (2 sticks)
- ¾ cup + 1 tablespoon granulated sugar
- ¾ cup packed light brown sugar
- 2 large eggs
- 1 ¼ teaspoons vanilla extract
- ¼ teaspoon freshly squeezed lemon juice
- 2 ¼ cups flour
- ½ cup rolled oats
- 1 teaspoon baking soda
- 1 teaspoon salt
- Pinch of cinnamon
- 2 2/3 cups of Nestlé Toll House semi-sweet chocolate chips
- 1 ¼ cups chopped walnuts
- ¼ to ½ cup raw sunflower seeds

Directions:

- Cream butter, sugar, and brown sugar in the bowl of a mixer on medium speed for two minutes.
- Add eggs, vanilla, and lemon juice, blending with a mixer on low speed for 30 seconds, then medium speed for two minutes or until light and fluffy, scraping down the bowl.
- With the mixer on low speed, add flour, oats, baking soda, salt, and cinnamon, blending for about 45 seconds. Don't overmix.
- Remove bowl from mixer and stir in chocolate chips and nuts.

- Portioned dough with a small scoop equal to about two tablespoons of mixture. Drop the mixture onto a baking sheet lined with parchment paper, spacing about 2 inches between scoops.

- Preheat oven to 300°F. Bake for 20 to 23 minutes, or until the edges are golden brown and the center is still soft.

- Remove from the oven and cool on a baking sheet for about one hour.

- You can freeze the unbaked cookie dough that was formed into individual balls. There's no need to thaw. Preheat oven to 300°F and place frozen cookies on a parchment paper-lined baking sheet about 2 inches apart. Bake until the edges are golden brown and the center is still soft.

Notes:

If you flatten the cookie dough into a 1-inch-thick sheet before freezing, you can cut the dough into one or 2-inch squares to bake rather than using a scooper.

Since all ovens vary, you may have to experiment with the time to achieve the crisp edges and soft interior. Suppose you have a convection oven that is the best. Just reduce the cooking time to 22 minutes. Be sure to let your cookies cool completely before testing.

Enough cooking, let's eat!

Top left: Salmon with Cherry Tomato Salsa, p. 31

Top right: Fish Tacos p. 45

Center: Hot Avocado and Shrimp Soup, p. 26, and Red Eye Oysters, p. 86

The above was served with an ice-cold adult beverage.

APPENDIX
Miscellaneous Useful Stuff

Blackened Fish

Over the years, I have subjected Mrs. to eating out at our local seafood restaurants just to make sure that what we cook at home is as good (or better) as they are doing. One area that we have found lacking in many restaurants is blackened seafood. Blackened foods are just meats that are seasoned and then cooked briefly at a very high heat. For those who want to know how to cook blackened fish, here is the way it should be done.

- Before you start, notify the local fire department and the company that is monitoring your alarm system that the smoke coming out of your house is from cooking and that it's not on fire. If you prepare this outdoors, which is the best place to do it, notify Homeland Security that you're not manufacturing bombs when a small mushroom cloud rises in the air from your cooking area.

- If possible, find a well-seasoned cast-iron frying pan or a heavy-duty stainless-steel pan. Do not use ceramic or aluminum pans as they tend to break or melt from the high heat.

- If your barbecue has a burner, it's best to heat your frying pan outside on the barbecue. You want to heat it at least to 400°+ before starting to cook. This step will often take 10 to 20 minutes to reach the correct temperature. We use one of those infrared thermometers to measure the heat. Wear welder's gloves or have heavy-duty potholders handy because the handles will get extremely hot. Having a fire extinguisher nearby won't hurt either. Then….

- Catch and fillet a fish or two into ½- to ¾-inch thick fillets (we like snapper, grouper, or dolphin).

- Select one of about 100 blackened seasonings on the market. We use Chef Paul Prudhomme's Blackened Redfish Magic, but almost any blackened seafood seasoning will work. And then…...

- Start heating your frying pan on high heat.

- In a separate container, melt a stick of unsalted butter over low heat.

- After about 10 or 15 minutes, your frying pan might be hot enough to start cooking. Just test with your infrared thermometer.

- Dip or brush each side of your fillets in the melted butter and season. Depending on the size of the fillet, put about a teaspoon or so of the seasonings on both sides. Another technique is to mix the seasoning in the melted butter before coating your fillet. Either way works well. Be aware that you should use more seasonings in the butter when you season your fillets that way.

- Now comes the fun; what you are going to do after dipping is throw the fish into the frying pan and retreat behind a barrier, just in case. Or at least stand back. The theory here is that when the butter hits the superheated pan, it turns into superheated steam, forcing the spices up into the flesh of the fish. This process produces a lot of smoke, so it's probably a good idea to serve some adult beverages to your guests before you start cooking and warn them that you're going to put on a show for them. Hopefully, you have notified the fire department and the neighborhood busybodies that you are cooking because it is very embarrassing to have the fire department show up and have to feed them because they went through all that trouble to come to your house to put out a fire.

- After about two or more minutes, depending on how thick the fillet is, it should slide freely into the frying pan. Now flip it over and again watch the smoke cloud rise over your home for another three or so minutes. If the fish slides freely, it's time to plate. Your fish should have a beautiful crust on both sides, be moist inside, and taste better than any restaurant-cooked fish you've ever had. (Note: Part of the problem with restaurants is that many do not get their pans as hot as they should be, and they usually only season one side).

Notes:

This gourmet dish can be served over a bed of long-grain rice or by itself. If you make biscuits and honey, you are in for a real treat. Oh, yes, the Mrs. said to remind you all to include some sort of healthy vegetable such as asparagus, corn sprinkled with Old Bay Seasoning, or mushrooms sautéed in garlic and butter.

Serve with some white wine.

P.S. This same technique will work well on steaks and chicken.

Grilling Fish

- While Chef Slavic used tilefish for his demonstration, the technique can be applied to almost any firm-fleshed fish you want to grill.

- First, place pieces for the grill in a pan. Sprinkle each piece with Kosher salt.

- Next, spray each piece with Pam on one side, usually the skin side, and place that side down on the grill.

- Cook the fish until it is flaky but still moist.

Serve with one of the following sauces.

Hollandaise Sauce

Ingredients:

- In preparation, melt one stick (¼ pound) of butter.

- Have ready a teaspoon of salt, ½ teaspoon of white pepper, and at least ¼ teaspoon of cayenne pepper.

- Separate four eggs at room temperature. Squeeze juice from ½ of a fresh lemon.

Directions:

- Start heating your water (hot but not boiling).

- Next, place the four egg yolks and the lemon juice in a pan or bowl resting on the hot (not boiling) water.

- Begin using a wire whisk (one of those fancy things with a bunch of wires on the end). Whisk really well to add air into the mixture.

- Gradually add the melted butter a little at a time and keep whisking.

- Finally, add a teaspoon of salt, the white pepper, and cayenne.

- Whisk everything until it is very, very smooth.

Note: *Mrs. and Iron Pot like our sauce with more tartness, so we add more lemon juice, a tablespoon at a time, to taste.*

Béarnaise Sauce

Using the same Hollandaise Sauce recipe above as the base….

Slowly add ½ cup warm heavy cream and one tablespoon chopped fresh tarragon leaves.

Hint one: Always add the fresh ingredients last to maintain a fresher flavor.

Hint two: Always make these sauces no more than 20 minutes before serving.

Iron Pot's hint: If you make both sauces, cover half the fish with one sauce and the other half of the fish with the other sauce. Keeps everyone guessing.

Here's an aside from Slavic on how to make an onion pie. Slice red onions as you would slice apples for a pie. Sauté them in butter over very low heat. Sprinkle the onions with brown sugar and serve on fish or veal. This adds a new dimension to the traditional preparation of standard dishes.

Current cooking philosophy: Most meats cook best when sprinkled with salt and pepper and sit for up to half an hour before cooking.

Notes:

Tartar Sauce

Ingredients:

- ½ cup real mayonnaise, not salad dressing
- 2 tablespoons finely chopped pickles (either sweet or dill pickles, according to taste)
- 1 tablespoon rice wine vinegar
- 1 tablespoon drained capers
- 1 teaspoon coarse-grained mustard
- About a pinch each of salt and pepper

Directions:

Throw everything into a bowl, mix well, and cover. Cool down the sauce for 10 minutes to let the ingredients get to know each other.

You may wish to adjust the various ingredients in the tartar sauce to suit your tastes. Remember, the cook defines what tastes good.

Notes: ____

____

____

____

____

Cajun Seasoning

Ingredients:

- ¼ cup coarse salt (Kosher or sea)
- 2 tablespoons garlic powder
- 2 tablespoons onion powder
- 2 tablespoons dried thyme
- 2 tablespoons dried oregano
- 2 tablespoons sweet paprika
- 1 tablespoon freshly ground black pepper
- 1 tablespoon freshly ground white pepper
- 1 to 3 teaspoons cayenne pepper (to taste)

Directions:

Use on meats and chicken. For fish see next bullets.

- Mix 1 ½ to 2 tablespoons of the above mixture with 1 ½ tablespoons of Old Bay Seasoning.
- Apply to your fish at least 30 minutes before grilling.
- This can be stored in an airtight jar in a dark place for up to 6 months.

Notes: ____

____

____

____

Shellfish Boil

Ingredients:

- ¼ cup mustard seeds
- ¼ cup coriander seeds
- 2 tablespoons dill
- 2 tablespoons whole allspice
- 1 tablespoon whole cloves
- 1 tablespoon dried hot peppers
- 3 medium-sized bay leaves finely crumbled

Directions:

One trick we learned from some "old-timers" is that to increase the intensity of the taste, particularly for shrimp and crawfish, turn off the heat after they have cooked for 2 to 3 minutes. Then, let the shellfish sit in the boil for 10 minutes.

Notes: _______________________________________

____

____

____

____

Our Basic Cupboard Stock at Home

- Sea salt and Kosher salt

- A good pepper grinder

- Olive Oil and Safflower cooking oil (Iron Skillet wanted me to cook healthier).

- Thyme, dill, parsley, and rosemary, fresh when available

- Fresh garlic cloves, garlic salt

- Both salted and unsalted butter

- Flour and cornmeal

- 4 or 5 different hot sauces, including Tabasco, Ghost Pepper, and Datil pepper sauces

- Of course, we use fresh items like lemons, limes, chives, and both yellow and red onions.

- To accompany our seafood meal, we like to keep on hand some cold beer, white wine, and soda water, as you never know who might drop in with some fresh fish that "just wants to be cooked." Tea, both sweet and regular, is another popular drink.

Notes: ____

____

____

____

____

Stocks: Fish, Chicken, and Vegetable

One of the most often used items in any stew-type dish is some sort of stock. I remember my parents saving turkey, chicken, and fish parts until they could make a stock. Then, they would freeze the stock in empty (and cleaned) Cool Whip bowls. Whenever my family needed a stock, the word was "check the freezer."

Here are some basic stock recipes we use. If you want more choices, just do a Google search for the type of stock you want. You should get about 10 zillion recipes. The key to the preparation of most stocks is to skim off the top layer produced while boiling. When cooking fish stock, there will be a froth. When making beef and chicken stock, there will be a fatty layer formed after the liquid cools down.

If you don't have time to make your own stock, you can find these broths in the form of bouillon or canned broth at your local market. However, nothing beats your fresh homemade stock.

Notes: ____

____

____

____

____

Fish Stock

Ingredients:

- 2 pounds of fish heads, bones, and trimmings from fish. If you don't have any leftovers from your fishing trip, your local fish market should have some. But call ahead just to be sure.

- 1 medium onion, sliced

- 2 celery stalks, chopped

- 1 carrot, sliced. Some recipes omit the carrot; it's your choice.

- ½ lemon, sliced. This is optional, but we like to use lemon.

- 1 or 2 bay leaves broken into smaller pieces

- 6 to 8 black peppercorns like you use in your pepper grinder

- 1 tablespoon chopped parsley, not the broad-leaf Italian kind

- 2 quarts of water. Use filtered water, if possible, to eliminate any

- chlorine taste.

- 2/3 cup dry white wine. You might have to taste several wines to find the right one.

Directions:

- Rinse all the fish parts well under cold running water. Then, put everything in your stock pot and bring it to a boil, skimming the surface frequently. Then, lower the temperature to a slow simmer for 25 minutes.

- Strain the stock through a fine strainer or several layers of cheesecloth. If you don't use it immediately, then you can cool it down in the refrigerator for use within 2 days. Otherwise, freeze it. It will last up to 3 months.

Notes: ____

____

____

____

____

Chicken Stock

A lot of times, you might have to use a chicken stock when you don't have a fish stock. But be careful; you might have to water it down some so that it doesn't overpower your fish dish. Trick: We use chicken stock to heat up our white meat turkey slices at Thanksgiving. We often get a lot of compliments on how juicy our turkey is…but that's our secret.

Ingredients:

- 2 ½ to 3 pounds chicken or turkey wings, backs, necks, and carcass. No gizzards or livers.
- 2 medium onions, quartered
- 1 tablespoon olive oil
- 2 carrots, sliced or chopped
- 2 celery stalks, chopped
- 1 tablespoon chopped parsley
- 2 sprigs of fresh thyme or ¾ teaspoon dried thyme. Don't forget to crush the dried leaves between your fingers to open up the flavor.
- 1 or 2 bay leaves broken into several pieces
- 10 black peppercorns. You may want to crack them a little to release their flavor.
- 4½ quarts of water. Use filtered water if possible to eliminate any chlorine taste.

Directions:

- Heat the olive oil on medium heat in your stockpot, then add the poultry parts and the onions. Cook, stirring occasionally, until everything is an even light brown.

- Add the water and scrape the bottom of the pot to get all the goodies on the bottom. Bring to a boil and skim off the impurities as they rise to the surface of the stock.

- Now add the rest of the ingredients, lower the heat, and simmer the stock for about 3 hours. You will want to partially cover the pot to increase the flavor and control evaporation.

- Using a fine mesh strainer or several layers of cheesecloth, strain the broth into a bowl to cool. Chill in the refrigerator for at least 1 hour. Once cooled down, gently skim off the layer of fat from the surface. This stock will be kept for several days or frozen until needed.

Notes: ____

____

____

____

____

Vegetable Stock

We don't use a lot of vegetable stock, but here's how we make it when needed. To do it right, you need to have a lot of ingredients, which is the other reason we don't make it often. That said, it really is a good-tasting stock.

Ingredients:

- 2 leeks (white and light green parts) roughly chopped
- 3 celery stalks, roughly chopped
- 1 large, chopped onion. We prefer Spanish or yellow onion.
- 2 fresh ½-inch cubes of ginger root chopped
- 1 yellow bell pepper, seeded and chopped
- 1 parsnip, chopped
- ½ cup fresh mushrooms, including stalks, sliced thickly
- 1 small seeded and chopped tomato
- 3 tablespoons light soy sauce
- 3 bay leaves
- A bunch of parsley stems. Cut off the tops and save them for later use.
- 2 or 3 sprigs of fresh thyme
- 1 sprig of rosemary
- 2 teaspoons salt
- Freshly ground pepper
- 3 ¼ cups water. Use filtered water, if possible, to eliminate the chlorine taste.

Directions:

- Put everything into your stock pot or large saucepan and bring to a boil. Then lower to a simmer for about 30 minutes.
- Cool first, and then strain. Your vegetable stock is now ready to use, or you can freeze it until needed.

Notes: ____

____

____

____

____

Nowadays, many people are excited about calories, cholesterol, and protein count. Here is a chart from the US Food and Drug Administration to help with those counts.

Seafood Nutrition Facts

Cooked (by moist or dry heat with no added ingredients), edible weight portion. Percent Daily Values (%DV) are based on a 2,000 calorie diet.

Seafood (Serving Size (84 g/3 oz))	Calories	Calories from Fat	Total Fat (g / %DV)	Saturated Fat (g / %DV)	Cholesterol (mg / %DV)	Sodium (mg / %DV)	Potassium (mg / %DV)	Total Carbohydrate (g / %DV)	Protein (g)	Vitamin A (%DV)	Vitamin C (%DV)	Calcium (%DV)	Iron (%DV)
Blue Crab	100	10	1 / 2	0 / 0	95 / 32	330 / 14	300 / 9	0 / 0	20g	0%	4%	10%	4%
Catfish	130	60	6 / 9	2 / 10	50 / 17	40 / 2	230 / 7	0 / 0	17g	0%	0%	0%	0%
Clams, about 12 small	110	15	1.5 / 2	0 / 0	80 / 27	95 / 4	470 / 13	6 / 2	17g	10%	0%	8%	30%
Cod	90	5	1 / 2	0 / 0	50 / 17	65 / 3	460 / 13	0 / 0	20g	0%	2%	2%	2%
Flounder/Sole	100	15	1.5 / 2	0 / 0	55 / 18	100 / 4	390 / 11	0 / 0	19g	0%	0%	2%	0%
Haddock	100	10	1 / 2	0 / 0	70 / 23	85 / 4	340 / 10	0 / 0	21g	2%	0%	2%	6%
Halibut	120	15	2 / 3	0 / 0	40 / 13	60 / 3	500 / 14	0 / 0	23g	4%	0%	2%	6%
Lobster	80	0	0.5 / 1	0 / 0	60 / 20	320 / 13	300 / 9	1 / 0	17g	2%	0%	6%	2%
Ocean Perch	110	20	2 / 3	0.5 / 3	45 / 15	95 / 4	290 / 8	0 / 0	21g	0%	2%	10%	4%
Orange Roughy	80	5	1 / 2	0 / 0	20 / 7	70 / 3	340 / 10	0 / 0	16g	2%	0%	4%	2%
Oysters, about 12 medium	100	35	4 / 6	1 / 5	80 / 27	300 / 13	220 / 6	6 / 2	10g	0%	6%	6%	45%
Pollock	90	10	1 / 2	0 / 0	80 / 27	110 / 5	370 / 11	0 / 0	20g	2%	0%	0%	2%
Rainbow Trout	140	50	6 / 9	2 / 10	55 / 18	35 / 1	370 / 11	0 / 0	20g	4%	4%	8%	2%
Rockfish	110	15	2 / 3	0 / 0	40 / 13	70 / 3	440 / 13	0 / 0	21g	4%	0%	2%	2%
Salmon, Atlantic/Coho/Sockeye/Chinook	200	90	10 / 15	2 / 10	70 / 23	55 / 2	430 / 12	0 / 0	24g	4%	4%	2%	2%
Salmon, Chum/Pink	130	40	4 / 6	1 / 5	70 / 23	65 / 3	420 / 12	0 / 0	22g	2%	0%	2%	4%
Scallops, about 6 large or 14 small	140	10	1 / 2	0 / 0	65 / 22	310 / 13	430 / 12	5 / 2	27g	2%	0%	4%	14%
Shrimp	100	10	1.5 / 2	0 / 0	170 / 57	240 / 10	220 / 6	0 / 0	21g	4%	4%	6%	10%
Swordfish	120	50	6 / 9	1.5 / 8	40 / 13	100 / 4	310 / 9	0 / 0	16g	2%	2%	0%	6%
Tilapia	110	20	2.5 / 4	1 / 5	75 / 25	30 / 1	360 / 10	0 / 0	22g	0%	2%	0%	2%
Tuna	130	15	1.5 / 2	0 / 0	50 / 17	40 / 2	480 / 14	0 / 0	26g	2%	2%	2%	4%

Seafood provides negligible amounts of trans fat, dietary fiber, and sugars.

U.S. Food and Drug Administration
(January 1, 2008)